UNTETHERED
SKY

FONDA LEE

UNTETHERED SKY

TOR PUBLISHING GROUP

NEW YORK

UNTETHERED SKY

Copyright © 2023 by Fonda Lee

A Tordotcom Book
Published by Tom Doherty Associates/Tor Publishing Group
120 Broadway
New York, NY 10271

www.tor.com

Tor® is a registered trademark of Macmillan Publishing Group, LLC.

The Library of Congress Cataloging-in-Publication Data
is available upon request.

ISBN 978-1-250-84246-6 (hardcover)
ISBN 978-1-250-84247-3 (ebook)

Our books may be purchased in bulk for promotional,
educational, or business use. Please contact your local bookseller
or the Macmillan Corporate and Premium Sales Department
at 1-800-221-7945, extension 5442, or by email at
MacmillanSpecialMarkets@macmillan.com.

First Edition: 2023

Printed in the United States of America

0 9 8 7 6 5 4 3 2 1

FOR SASHA,

My writing companion and a very good dog

I

FLEDGLING

Zahra was her name. When the crate opened, all I saw at first were her eyes, the largest of any living creature, enormous golden orbs fixing me with a raptor's murderous glare. She was a year-old fledgling taken from the nest, already lethal and immense. I was a woman of eighteen, small, wounded, overanxious. Sweat coated my hands and lathered my body beneath heavy leather work gloves and a tarnished scale vest. Ruhkers have been killed on the first day. If it happened to me, another apprentice would take my place.

Zahra stepped calmly into the mews pen without coaxing. Babak and the gathered ruhkers watching from behind the bars nodded approvingly. The fledgling hadn't hunched in the crate in fear, nor exploded out of it screaming with rage. She was healthy, calm, and brave—the most anyone could ask for. My excitement ran like a fever—the blood hot in my head, my fingertips tingling and swollen. I was thrillingly, terrifyingly aware of my fragility. A roc could knock me down in a single blow. With one massive taloned foot, she could crush my head like a ripe apricot and tear out my entrails before anyone could make a move.

I loved her with the gravity of a stone sinking into a pool.

A fully grown female roc stands a head taller than most men. Fully spread, her wings reach as wide as three people lined up fingertip to fingertip with arms outstretched. Rocs aren't the impossible size that storytellers and artists would have you believe, but nevertheless Zahra loomed over me. She made the falcon I'd flown as a girl seem like a toy.

I began to speak quietly, murmuring my admiration for her as I picked up the butchered hind leg of a boar, careful to use my nondominant hand as I placed it on the wooden perch. Zahra's head jerked, staring first at me, then at my offering. A moment of fateful decision— one that felt to me like the judgment of God—before she hopped onto the perch as if she'd done it a thousand times and began to tear into the meat.

Audible sighs of relief escaped those watching. I backed out of the mews, opening and closing one barred gate and then the other, my knees weak. Babak was counting out a fat purse of silver for Gazsi, the roc hunter. He handed over the payment grudgingly but without complaint. As Master of the Royal Mews, Babak was responsible for ensuring that the king's rocs and the ruhkers who handled them were maintained at full roster and in good condition. Gazsi charged a fortune for a captured fledgling, but as one of the few reliable roc hunters, he could do so.

Gazsi sauntered past, whistling and swinging the bulging bag of coins. He paused beside me. "She was second to hatch." The roc hunter's voice was gruff, but had the singsong quality of a man from the mountain tribes. "Her sister tried to kill her, to push her out of the nest, but she hung on. I was going to take the older chick, but then I saw this one start to fly. She flew farther and faster than the other one. Was the first to hunt, the first to make a kill."

He seemed almost teary-eyed—an incongruous sight, as Gazsi was a lion of a man, with a mane of wild hair and so many roc-inflicted scars that he looked as if he'd been flogged in a dozen dungeons. Roc hunters are even more demented than ruhkers. Gazsi spent months scaling the steepest peaks in search of roc eyries. If he found a nest, he camped in hiding nearby, watching the ugly white chicks until they grew into sleek dark youths and could fly and hunt on their own. Then he set a baited net trap in hopes of capturing and subduing a fledgling while its parents were away or not paying attention. So many things could go wrong: The trap might fail, leaving him with nothing to show for the season. The angry, trapped roc might kill or maim him. The adults might discover him and tear him to pieces, feeding him to the same chicks he'd watched hatch and grow.

Gazsi looked down at me, his nostrils flaring. His expression suggested he didn't think I was worthy of the roc he'd risked his life to bring to the mews. Perhaps he held that opinion of every new ruhker. "Camel meat is her favorite. Liver especially." He jingled his bag of money and strode away.

"Ester!" Nasmin came over and embraced me. When she pulled back, she kept ahold of my shoulders, her eyes dancing with excitement and the covetousness that every ruhker has when a new roc arrives. Ruhkers can't get enough of rocs. Even with their own to occupy them, they can't help jealously admiring new fledglings. "She's splendid," Nasmin declared. "I can't wait until we're hunting together. I'll bring you all the choice bits from Azar's kills during your dark days."

I nodded in wordless thanks, relaxing a little into her optimism. Most ruhkers paid little attention to the apprentices, but Nasmin was one of the younger women in the mews and one of the few who'd been kind to me when I'd arrived a year ago. The simple knowledge that I had a friend who'd gone through what I was facing and was confident in my survival made it easier to not think about the alternative.

Babak handed me a canteen of water, a sack full of raw meat, and a blanket for when night fell. The Master of the Mews was nearly forty, a veritable ancient by ruhkers' standards. His face was square and sun-leathered, his beard closely trimmed, and he spoke with gestures, grunts, and frowns more than words. Babak never treated me better or worse than any other apprentice. Only competence and dedication to one's bird meant anything to him.

When a ruhking apprenticeship opens, each satrapy in the realm is required to submit the name of one candidate between the ages of sixteen and twenty-two, with talent in hunting, tracking, riding, and falconry, among other qualities. When I'd presented myself in the governor's receiving room to ask for the nomination, Governor Govad had frowned down at me with grandfatherly bewilderment and concern. "Ruhking is no fit life for a young woman." Govad had tugged doubtfully on his thick beard. "If you succeed, you won't be able to come home. If you fail, you certainly won't be able to come home." In the end, however, he nominated me, perhaps because I continued to plead my case no matter his attempts to dissuade me. Or perhaps there were no better or more willing candidates.

Out of every five apprentice ruhkers, two will be killed or maimed, two will leave or be sent away, and only one will ever fly a roc. And the dangers do not diminish after that. Babak had seen apprentices come and go. He would place no odds on my success, yet his equanimity was an odd comfort, because I shared his blunt assessment: Either I would become a ruhker, or I would die trying. I would train and care for Zahra, yet she could never belong to me. In name, she belonged to Antrius the Bold and the Kingdom of Dartha, but even that was not true. A roc is always a wild thing, always God's monster alone.

"Five days dark, then hood her," Babak said. "I want her up in the air by next month, which means no time to waste backtracking on training if you make mistakes. Do it right."

I tilted my face toward the sky, trying to soak in

enough sunlight to carry me through the days to come. Then I went into the pen to join my splendid monster in darkness.

I was six years old the first time I saw a roc. At first, I thought it was an especially large buzzard circling overhead, but then it drifted lower in the sky, and I saw the shape and color of it, the sheer *size* of it. I started running, laughing and shouting, toward the open ground beneath where it balanced on the stiff wind. I wasn't afraid, just childishly delighted, as if I'd seen a horse the size of a tree, or a dog the size of an ox.

My mother grabbed me by the arm with a shriek. "Holy fires, it'll think you're a little monkey and carry you right off!"

That was nonsense. Rocs don't carry their prey away, and trained rocs don't attack humans, but my mother didn't know that. Nevertheless, she was right that it's a bad idea to run underneath a hunting roc and distract it with noise and movement; ruhkers hate it when people do that.

Wild rocs were a rare sight in the south where I grew up. My father was a minor landowner with a small but fertile and well-managed parcel of pastureland upon which we raised goats and grew olive trees. We weren't wealthy, but we were well off enough to have house servants in addition to field serfs. After I was born, it seemed my mother wasn't able to have more children. She miscarried several times, each loss causing her tremendous pain and heartache. In some of my earliest memories, she's lying on cushions, sweaty, pale, and exhausted, her breath sour from throwing up. "You were too big and came out too late," she moaned. "You ruined something inside me."

My parents went to the Fire Temple and fed sticks of sandalwood to the holy flames, they consulted with magi and astronomers, my father sacrificed many bulls and gave money to the poor, my mother sought out a slew of midwives and physicians, even journeying for days to see specialists in Antopolis, trying every medicine or remedy. But by the time I was eight years old, my parents had given up on their dreams of having a large family.

"Ester," my mother said, "you're a miracle. You're our one and only. Don't ever get married, don't ever leave your father and me alone." Even though she was a sad and unhealthy woman, my mother was still sweet to me. She was undemanding, generous to the servants, and didn't make a fuss over getting things done in a certain way or by a certain time. She thought life ought to be enjoyed in the moment, messiness tolerated, and even children and slaves should feel free to sing and dance.

My father's desire for a son was so strong that he not only allowed but encouraged me in the things I most loved to do: wandering for hours, getting dirty exploring, riding my mule, and looking after all sorts of animals, from baby goats to injured birds. He took me along as he made the rounds of our property, speaking to the senior field hands about irrigation, and crop yield, and fences against the wolves. I loved our land: the pale green grazing fields in the valley by the creek, the tidy groves of sunbaked black olive trees in red dirt, the mist that sometimes rolled down from the blue shadow of the mountains, and the gigantic sky, upon which only a few stretched clouds loitered.

Then, a miracle: My mother became pregnant. My parents were afraid to be too hopeful; after all, my mother had lost babies in their fifth month. So they prayed earnestly but quietly and tiptoed on cosmic eggshells, trying to pad our lives with good deeds in the hopes that this time their efforts would be noticed and rewarded. My father held a summer feast for three hundred people and gave our servants time off to visit their relatives. My mother did healthful breathing exercises and drank special soups and admonished me if I ever so much as muttered an unkind word about anything.

All their fervent wishing paid off. I was nine years old when my brother, Arnan, was born.

Arnan was a fussy, temperamental baby, but my parents were so overjoyed with him that even his hours of incessant bawling didn't dent their enthusiasm. The whole house would be kept awake during his colicky nights, but if, in my sleep-deprived clumsiness the next morning, I happened to drop a bowl on the floor, my mother would hiss at me to be quiet and not wake the baby.

You can't blame me for not being as thrilled with Arnan as my parents were. When he was in a good mood, he could be a charming little fellow. He would run up and hug me, and I would hold him on my lap and play with him and tell him stories, feeling very much like a responsible big sister.

Most other times, though, I felt driven to slip away to where I felt most at ease and most myself: wandering alone in the wide, quiet spaces, searching out birds' nests, picking wild figs, stirring the creek bed with my bare feet.

I had a falcon, a male saker I named Cas, and I trained him to hunt birds. He was small and unusually light in color, quick off the glove and beautiful to watch, cream and dappled brown, like milk sprinkled with cinnamon. We had some open fields at the edge of our property that were ideal for flying him. One cool morning in the spring, I walked out to see a chariot standing in the tall grass. I was in a sour mood; my mother had told me to be back in an hour because I had to watch Arnan today, as she was going into town to shop for spices. So I could only get a couple flights in, at best. But the sight of the chariot made me forget everything. It looked like it might be a nobleman's war chariot. Sunlight winked off the rims of its wheels as if they were giant golden coins, and its sides were painted with red feathers on a shining black background. The two harnessed stallions had proud arching necks and flowing white manes. There was a figure standing in the chariot, one hand shielding his eyes as he tilted his head back and scanned the sky. He blew a shrill reed whistle: *tweee tweeeeee.*

I walked closer and he noticed me. I stopped, Cas sitting hooded on my fist, as I stared into the face of a young man with a jet-black beard and dimples over his eyebrows. For a long moment, we eyed each other curiously. "That's a good-looking tiercel you have," he said. "I bet he's got fire. How long have you been flying him?"

"Since last year," I said. And then because the young man seemed friendly, and knew something about falcons, I asked, "Are you a falconer too?"

The young man laughed, a musical sound. "I don't hunt *sparrows*." He looked up into the sky once more. I followed his gaze and saw the vast silhouette of a roc swooping toward us, wings spread, just the tips of the long flight feathers moving as she sailed in a long, curving arc, nearly skimming the ground at the end of her trajectory. I ducked as she brought her flight up short, her huge taloned feet reaching seemingly for my head. A single one of them could encircle my skull the way a man might pluck a peach. She went right past me, the wind in her wake buffeting me in the face like a flash gale, here and gone in an instant. With astonishing silence, she landed on the chariot cadge, calm and regal as a queen.

Her ruhker tossed her a piece of meat the size of my fist, then hooded her and leashed her jesses. Up close, her size and beauty stole my breath; she didn't seem as if she could be real. In some of the magi's stories, angels take the form of rocs to convey the immortal souls of heroes to the spirit realm. In that moment, I believed it utterly. Yet the ruhker moved around her with ease and complete lack of fear, as if going through a familiar routine with an old friend. When he was done, he took up his spot in the chariot. He glanced back at me, touching his fore-head briefly in greeting and farewell. "Good hunting." He flicked the reins, sending the horses forward.

I watched until the pair of figures, the man and the roc, vanished behind a dip in the land. Then I turned around and ran back home without even flying Cas, my heart thumping. I wished I could've run after the chariot and shouted for it to wait for me. I imagined the ruhker holding his hand out to me, so I could take it and jump up beside him and go to whatever wondrous place it was where people and giant birds lived together.

Heavy canvas covered the gate and window of Zahra's pen, blocking out the sunlight and noise of the outside world. During my waking hours, I walked slowly around the enclosure, my hand trailing the wall, talking to Zahra in a calm, low tone. I heard her shifting on the perch, ruffling her feathers.

The dark days acclimate the roc to the ruhker's voice and presence. In the long period of sensory deprivation, the fledging starts to forget her old life, to feel that per-haps she has always been in this dark room, that the voice of her trainer is the only constant, the only thing there is, the only thing there ever will be.

It does the same to the ruhker. As the hours and then the days passed, my life shrank to nothing but Zahra. I marked the passage of time only by the regular occasions when the corner of the drape would lift and a hand would pass me a fresh canteen of water and a small meal—kebab wrapped in flatbread, a bowl of rice or stew, a piece of fruit. A few times it was Nasmin's hand that reached through the bars. She squeezed my fingers in wordless support and passed me damp packages wrapped in cloth—the liver of a jackal, the heart of a wolf, the lungs of a wild pig.

I fed these delicacies to Zahra. I parsed out her food sparingly, so it was never long before she felt hungry again. It was important that she view me as a source of food as many times as possible during this impressionable period. Humans are not the preferred prey of rocs, but with a strong enough appetite and opportunity, they're not picky. I had to prove to my roc that I was a better provider than I was a meal.

Sometimes a young roc is not convinced. I'm glad I wasn't at the scene last month when screaming erupted from inside the mews and the canvas was drawn back on one of the new fledglings, mantled over her ruhker, eating his entrails.

Zahra became accustomed to the sound and shape of me moving around the pen, bringing tasty treats to her perch. It was not entirely dark in the room after our eyes adjusted. Light seeped in between the cracks of the wooden-plank walls and around the edges of the draping, just enough to see by. I paid close attention to how eagerly she fed; I couldn't let her get too hungry or too full. While she ate, I ran my hands down her wings and back, admiring the sleekness of her feathers, teaching her to accept my touch. I felt a little sick with fear every time I approached her, but my voice did not waver from a soothing monotone. I was careful never to walk slower or faster, or to let my hands and body shake or fidget. All those things would've been signs of weakness, glaring evidence that I was just another prey animal.

On the second or third day, a loud noise came from outside—perhaps a cart fell over—and Zahra startled, opening her wings and lifting off from her perch. She knocked me into a wall and I slid to the ground as if I'd been thrown. There was only room for her to flap a few times from one end of the enclosure to the other. By then the noise had stopped, and she settled down, but my head kept ringing for a while. Another time, I waited a bit too long with the next meal, and Zahra grabbed for the meat in my left hand as I moved it toward her perch. One of her talons tore through the thick leather of my glove and gave me a bloody gash on the forearm. Tears sprang to my eyes. I dropped the meat on the perch and, as she ate, I pulled off the glove and sucked the wound, silencing a whimper as I retreated to a corner. I could leave the mews if it was a matter of life or death, or I could reach behind the bars to pull a rope that would ring a bell for urgent help. I did neither. The cut wasn't deep. I wrapped it tightly in the cloth that had carried the still-warm wolf's heart.

Ruhkers must be endlessly patient, determined, and stoic. They can't express frustration, anger, or pain around their charges. During his apprenticeship, one of the other young ruhkers, Darius, had his arm broken by a roc while he was tethering it. He passed the leash to his other hand, tied it one-handed, and finished his chores cleaning the mews, sweeping with his right arm while his left hung dangling. All the while he never made a sound. After Darius's arm healed, Babak gave him the next roc to train.

I relieved myself in a straw-filled chamber pot and received one change of clothes through the bars. I drank water from my canteen in small sips every few minutes, but even so I wore my throat down. Ruhkers can barely talk at all after the dark days. What I said was not important, only the sound of my voice. So I told Zahra about how long I had been waiting for her. I told her about the other rocs and ruhkers in her new home. I told her about our future, about how we would always hunt together. I told her everything about my family and the place I grew up: olive trees and goats, the stone house, creek water ice-cold from the mountains, falcons waiting on above. Mother and Father and Arnan. When boredom and exhaustion turned my constant talk into babbling nonsense and dragged my chin to my chest, I slept.

I became convinced that Zahra was listening to me, that she understood and accepted me, that she would always hold in confidence my innermost thoughts and secrets. She would never question my purpose or examine my motives; for her, I simply *was*. An immovable aspect of her world, as she was now in mine. That is the true purpose of the dark days. Perhaps training a roc can be done in other ways, but shocking a person into the mindless devotion of a ruhker cannot.

When Arnan was four years old he was insufferably stubborn and demanding. My mother, who'd never been a robust woman to begin with, often suffered from back pain and leg cramps that sometimes caused her to lie in bed most of the day. Even with seemingly boundless reserves of indulgence for her precious son, she regularly told me to take him away for a few hours to give her some peace.

One morning I told Arnan we were going to the east pasture because there were new goat kids and I wanted to see them. He declared that would be boring and refused to go. What did he want to do then? He wanted to look for stones. Arnan had a collection of colorful creek stones that he carried around with him in a small leather sack. He was a little miser about those rocks, always taking them out and sorting them, polishing them, piling them in different groups, and putting them back in, like a moneylender counting his silver.

I made Arnan a deal. I'd play with him and his rocks for a while if he would then agree to go see the goats with me. And he would have to walk fast, because he was too big for me to carry and I had a lot of chores to do later. He agreed. Partway through the game, he realized he was missing one of his white rocks, which elicited a stamping tantrum. He ordered me to help him search in the grass for it, and when we couldn't find it, he demanded we go to the creek to look for a new white rock to replace the lost one. I refused, and started walking to the pastures. Arnan trailed after me, yelling at me to stop and turn back. I was the worst sister, a stupid girl, it was my job to take care of him, Mama said so. And so on. I kept walking. I heard him turn around and run back toward the house, howling with every step. *Good riddance,* I thought.

Arnan's voice didn't seem to be receding at all even though I was walking away as fast as I could. Finally, his screams cut out, presumably because he'd run inside to complain about me, and I closed my eyes at the bliss. The bees droned again. The birds chirped once more.

I sighed and turned around. My parents would not be impressed if I ran off for the rest of the day when I'd agreed to watch him. Since he'd calmed down, perhaps I could bribe him to forget his rocks and come along peacefully. I hurried back down the road and before I saw the house come into view, I saw *it* instead.

It was crouched like an enormous cat, elbows and hip bones jutting sharply out from its stocky frame, the quill-like hairs of its mottled pelt raised like a forest of needles. Its apelike head was bent low and I stared into its demonic face: malevolent mismatched eyes, slitted nostrils, a short grinning muzzle filled with two rows of dagger-teeth. The spiked mace-like tip of its tail whipped back and forth, lazily, in an arch over its body.

I had never seen one before, but countless frightening children's stories gave me the name at once: *manticore.*

At the manticore's feet was Arnan's embroidered red silk jacket. Inside the jacket, I knew in an instant of detached horror, was Arnan. The manticore's black tongue snaked out and licked his face, almost like a dog. Then it picked him up by his throat and stood, and my brother's body dangled limp from the manticore's jaws, the neck bent at an impossible angle, feet swinging just over the ground, one sandaled and one bare.

A scream began to leave my lips, but my fist, as if moving on its own, shoved itself into my mouth. I cut my knuckles on my teeth, tasted blood on my tongue just as my bladder gave out.

Run!

Arnan!

The two words shrieked in my mind at the same time and crashed, like two of my brother's warring stones flung into each other, meeting in midair with equal force, falling. Piss warmed the insides of my legs and between my toes, but I was frozen, frozen like a rabbit in an eagle's shadow, frozen as the breath before death. The manticore turned its gaze on me. One long, infinite stare. Its eyes resembled human eyes, but whatever feeling or intelligence was behind them was alien and hungry. One iris was golden brown, the other was as blue as the sky.

In the endless second when I knew my brother was dead and I was soon to join him, the door to my house opened and my mother came outside with a pitcher in one hand. "Arnan!" she called. "Ester—" She dropped the pitcher and screamed. Her scream split the air like axe cleaving bone.

The bronze pitcher landed and rolled away from her, spilling a river of white goat's milk. *No . . .* My brain seemed to be moving too slowly, far slower than everything else around me.

The manticore was not slow. It dropped Arnan and took three great bounds away from me, its body coiling and uncoiling with terrible grace, and on its third bound, it knocked my poor mother to the ground. Her skirt billowed and flapped between the manticore's front paws and her scream died in the air the instant she did.

My legs unlocked. They connected to the part of me that understood it was prey, the part that wanted to live. As the manticore shouldered through the open door of my house, the servants inside began to scream, and I ran for my life.

The well. I reached the well and rolled over the stone lip, bruising my hips. Hanging on with shaking arms, I scraped the skin off my knees and feet, scrabbling for a hold on the curved inside wall. My toes jammed into a crevice and I stifled a cry as one of the nails bent backward. A handhold, another foothold. A childhood spent climbing trees and scrambling up and down rocky embankments—*I could do this.* I could still hear screaming, which meant the manticore was not coming for me, not yet. I concentrated only on lowering myself, one inch at a time, to the bottom of the well.

My arms were fraying cord. At last I was low enough

that my foot could almost stretch down to the surface of the water. How deep was it? Not deep, it couldn't be—the spring had been drier than usual, nearly gone already. I pushed off the wall and dropped the rest of the way, legs buckling like a colt's as I landed in the knee-high water and fell onto my tailbone with a splash. I curled into a sitting ball, wrapping my arms around myself, and leaned my head on the wall, my mouth stretched wide in silent sobs.

There was no more screaming from above, no more sounds at all. Manticores are driven into a killing frenzy by the sound of screaming. As long as it hears screaming, the manticore will not stop to feed—it will keep killing, one person after another, until it's eliminated the threat of its prey fighting back and has enough food to gorge on until it's full for a month. The sudden quiet meant everyone was dead.

Long minutes passed, and then a shadow darkened the opening of the well. I didn't move. I didn't even raise my head to look up at it. If the magi are to be believed, the manticore resembles its master, and I didn't want the last thing I saw to be the face of the Deceiver. The manticore made a low snuffling sound as it paced a circle around the perimeter of the well. I squeezed my eyes shut and didn't breathe. I made myself as small and motionless as I could.

I'm not here. I'm not here. I'm not here.

The manticore thrust its head into the well, blotting out the light. It growled in frustration. One paw swiped the air above my head, then retreated. It couldn't reach me to drag me out and it couldn't climb in after me. I felt its hot breath seeping down the walls and tickling the back of my neck. Then it pulled away. A shaft of sun drilled down to the bottom of the well and sliced across my face and arm. I knew the manticore was gone. It was eating my family and dragging away the rest to enjoy later.

I don't know how long I stayed in the well. After some indeterminable time had passed, I thought about trying to climb back up, thinking that if I did, I would find everything as it had been—the day undisturbed, my mother turning to scoldingly ask me where I'd been all this time. We'd heard of manticore attacks, but they were rare in our area, something to be vaguely frightened of, yet easily dismissed, as unpredictable and unlikely as a lightning strike on one's house. I'd spent countless hours wandering alone in nature and never imagined it would betray me.

The sound of men's voices and horses woke me from the sleep that claims you after terror shuts you down. In a cracked voice I shouted, "Help! Please help me, I'm down here!" People came. They lowered ropes and pulled me from the well. The only thing I remember clearly after that is my father's hands, bloodstained, but his face, bloodless, shock having turned it as blank as a fresh piece of papyrus. His lips moved and formed my name, though no sound came out, and as I fell into his arms weeping, I saw and felt, for an instant, the grief-stricken question flash across his eyes and stiffen his frame.

Why her? Why did she have to be the one who lived?

I don't suppose my father ever guessed that I asked it as

endlessly as he did. Some say ruhking is a calling. For me it was an answer to a question that had bored clear through my soul. I had a hole worn through my center, like one of Arnan's interesting blue river stones. People have admired rocs for centuries. Artists paint them, sculpt them, tell stories about them. I wanted to *be* one. I wanted to be the monster that kills other monsters.

The dark days ended on the sixth morning, with a heavy rustle of canvas draping, a stinging shaft of dust-filled sunlight, Babak's voice. "It's time."

He handed me a beautiful leather hood, deep crimson, intricately tooled with patterns of flame and gold-colored stitching. Black leather braces jutted from the back and the crown of the hood flared in an ornate yellow and red tassel. I didn't want to sully it with my hands, dirty and stinking of organ meat.

Zahra was hunched on the perch, her golden eyes staring but unalert, sunken, as I was, into the monotony of darkness and eating. But she was hungry; she followed the motion of my left hand as I placed the bit of camel meat on the perch, then lowered her head. The tidbit disappeared into her crop, and as she straightened, I slipped the hood over her head and pulled the braces to tighten it.

She went motionless with confusion. My constant voice, however, and my hands stroking her wings—those were familiar things now. As Babak drew away the draping and fresh air flooded into the mews, she lifted her head and stood erect, opening her wings partway to feel the breeze.

Babak fastened anklets and jesses made of elephant hide to her legs. He attached the leash and tied it to the perch. It all happened quickly. "You can go now."

I felt at a loss. Isolation had brought my emotions frothing to the surface and I thought I might start to cry. I made my way to the ruhkers' house, swaying and filthy and empty-headed, a released prisoner. Where was Nasmin? I'd hoped she would be here to brightly reassure me that everything would be fine, that I was doing all right, that Zahra really was as beautiful and promising as I thought she was.

Instead, waiting on the path to the ruhkers' quarters was Darius. Two years older than me, skinny as a heron, the apprentice I remembered for having endured a broken arm with such aplomb. "Nasmin's been sent on a hunting call," he told me. "She'll be gone for eight days, maybe more. She asked me to tell you."

"Oh." Disappointment hunched my shoulders. Bone-deep fatigue hit me then. It was all I could do not to lie down on the path.

Darius appeared unsure of whether he was now free to walk away, his message delivered. He seemed ill at ease in conversation, one those ruhkers more comfortable with wild animals than other people. I couldn't remember the last time we'd exchanged more than a few words in politeness. "I saw her that first day," he said. "Your roc. She's beautiful."

When Darius said it, it was not the way an enthusiastic relative would compliment a baby, not the way Nasmin would say it. Darius said it the way a sculptor judges a statue, the way a chariot maker admires a fine new vehicle. "I think she'll be strong. Look at how large her feet are; you can tell she's still got growth. Good color. Nice and calm, too. She'll be a great bird, if she's not too lazy."

I wasn't sure if "thank you" was the right way to respond to such an assessment, so I nodded.

Darius rocked back and forth on his feet. "Minu is recovering from a bruised foot. I won't be flying her until it's better, so I'll be around. If you want help." I assumed his offer was made in politeness, since he walked past me without waiting for an answer.

The next morning, however, when I arrived back at the mews rested, fed, and washed, he was there.

"Are you waiting for someone?" I asked as I opened the gate to Zahra's pen.

"I wanted a better look at your roc. All I got was a glimpse that first day. I could help you with lure training, if you want."

"Her name's Zahra," I told him. I didn't dislike Darius, but I found him awkward, his quiet presence subtly judgmental. "I think I'll be fine without help."

He nodded, neither offended nor dissuaded. "Then I'd like to watch, if you don't mind."

Like most ruhkers, Darius's obsession with rocs was constant and insatiable. His own bird being grounded for the time being, he couldn't resist an opportunity to get close to a new one. An untrained, untested roc held such a magnetic draw that I suspected Darius might not be the only ruhker who'd come by to see how Zahra was progressing.

I put him out of my mind and stepped through the gate, closing it firmly behind me, leaving him on the other side of the bars. "Hello, my beautiful lady," I said quietly. "Did you sleep as well as I did last night? You must be hungry." Zahra tilted her head at the sound of my voice and raised her wings. They cast an enormous shadow across the enclosure.

"Easy, easy," I murmured, slowly running my hand across her upper covert feathers and down the long primaries. Seeing her properly now, in full daylight, Zahra took my breath away. She was still in her juvenile plumage: her breast a pale, speckled gray; her head, body, and wings dusky reddish-brown. Over the next couple of years, she would lose her mottling; her chest would become the pure white of harsh sunlight, and the rest of her would be the desert red of evening sun spilling across sand. Each of her great yellow toes ended in a sickle claw larger than a lion's fang. She was a perfect aerial killer. I couldn't wait to get her into the sky.

I stuffed down my impatience as I reached for a tidbit. Hurried or sloppy training would ruin her as a hunter and make her too dangerous to handle. Taking her out too early would mean losing her; she would simply fly off at the first opportunity, disappearing behind a treeline or over a ridge of scrubby horizon, never to be seen again.

Like Babak had said, I had to do it right. I drew out a piece of camel liver and pulled off her hood.

She looked around with jerky-headed curiosity, then noticed the bit of meat I'd placed on her perch. She swallowed it, then looked for more. I tried to put the hood back on, but she moved her head to avoid it, so I put a small piece of meat inside the hood and let her take it. As soon as she did, I slipped the hood back over her head. I waited a couple of minutes, then removed the hood and fed her another tidbit. She would learn to accept the hood with ease, to understand that every time it came off, she would be fed. I repeated the process—hood on, wait, hood off, offer tidbit—over and over. Training a roc is nothing if not repetitive.

After a while, I brought out the lure—a stuffed wolf-skin, head and tail still attached. Wolves would be her easiest quarry and most likely what we would start out hunting. I tied the rest of her meal to the lure and draped it over her perch, letting Zahra feed to her satisfaction while I cleaned out her pen. It takes a while to clean up after a man-sized bird. I was hot and tired under the armor and gloves by the time I was done. I mucked out her droppings, hung her hood on a nearby hook, added water to her bath, laid straw down under her perch, and raked the sand and gravel floor.

At some point, Darius left without me noticing.

He was back the next day when I continued introducing the hood and the lure, and the day after that. I started placing the lure some distance away from Zahra's perch.

When she jumped down on it, I blew a reed whistle and let her eat off the wolfskin. Then I put meat on her perch and whistled when she jumped back. Lure to perch, perch to lure. A few days later, I brought a chariot into her pen.

Rather, I tried. A two-man chariot is heavier than it looks, with large wheels that are difficult to maneuver unless you're a horse. Darius found me straining against it, pushing it infuriatingly slowly over to the mews. For a moment, he stood watching me. I must've been quite a sight.

"A little help?" I panted at last, hating him.

"I'm glad you asked," he said. "I wasn't sure if your pride or your back would give out first." He took hold of one wheel while I took the other. Together we rolled it into Zahra's pen.

I leaned over with a hand on one thigh, wiping my brow. Darius closed the gate and stood in front of it. I realized this was the first time he'd been on this side of the bars, inside Zahra's pen with me. I braced myself to feel annoyed, territorial. Instead I was pleased someone else was seeing Zahra up close. I hadn't realized how much I wanted to show her off.

I unhooded her and stepped back quickly.

Zahra lowered her head and hissed at the chariot box. Her beak opened wide, her shoulders went up, her feathers rose, making her seem even more gigantic. Even the largest lion would turn tail and run at her warning display. I flattened myself against the wall. For the first time, the primitive part of my brain recoiled at being trapped inside a room with this predator.

She lunged. The leash tethering her jesses to the heavy perch brought her up short, so she landed in front of the colorful chariot, not quite able to reach it. Instead, she rose up to her full fearsome height, stretching her legs and neck, and her enormous wings whipped forward and beat the sides and wheels of the chariot with shocking *thwap! thwap!* blows that would've pulverized a man's bones.

This went on for a couple of minutes before Zahra suddenly lost interest. It was as if, when the chariot didn't respond to her attack, she abruptly decided it was entirely unimportant and no longer worth a fraction of her attention. She hopped back onto her perch and ate from the lure, no longer sparing the chariot a glance.

I let out my breath. My legs were trembling. I looked over at Darius, still standing near the doors. He met my eyes, smiling more widely than I'd thought him capable of. "Fantastic," he mouthed.

I smiled back, my heart singing. She *was* fantastic.

When Zahra was done with the meat on the lure and was questing around for more, I untied her leash. I made my way over to the chariot box. A ruhker's chariot is a modified version of a light, two-man war chariot; there is room for the ruhker and one other person to stand, but unlike a normal chariot, the floor is longer and the back of the carriage is outfitted with a cadge, a travel perch upon which the roc stands and rides. I placed the hindquarters of a jackal on the chariot floor by the cadge and whistled. Zahra looked at me. I whistled again, and she jumped from her perch to the chariot cadge in one enormous bound.

Without preamble, she pinned the jackal's hindquarters with one foot and tore off an entire leg. She tilted it down her throat—bones, fur, claws, and all.

I wanted to dance and shout with excitement. I could call my roc to the chariot cadge! This action would be the basis of our entire partnership. I was one step closer to the day when I could call her down from the sky or off a kill. Every time Zahra returned to the chariot to be fed, she would be willingly forsaking the wild to hunt with me another day.

Darius saw my triumphant thoughts clear as the sky. He still wore a faint smile as we left Zahra to her meal. As we walked back to the ruhkers' house, I was so giddy, I forgot to maintain the indifference I'd been cultivating toward him. "Was that all right?" I blurted.

"Yes," he said, so quickly I knew it was true. "Everyone feels like they don't know what they're doing at the start. You're doing fine."

He started to walk away from me, and all of a sudden, I didn't want him to. "Wait," I said. He turned around. "You've been watching my roc every day. It's only fair I get to watch yours. When Minu's foot is better and she can hunt again, I'd like to . . . I mean, would you . . ." Embarrassingly, I found myself stumbling over my words. "Can I come along on one of her hunts?"

It would be some time before I could take Zahra on a hunt of her own. But I wanted to be out there already, squinting up into the sky and across the horizon, riding across those wild plains with a roc in the air above. I wanted to be a better partner for Zahra when she was ready.

This time, Darius did pause for a long moment to consider before answering. Long enough for me to regret asking. I was on the verge of saying, a little angrily, "Never mind then," when Darius said, "Would the day after tomorrow be too soon?"

We went out before dawn. Sunrise and dusk are when the big predators are most active and the best times to be ruhking. It was still full dark as Darius led the chariot up to the mews. I was yawning as I held the harnessed horses steady. Darius opened the doors to Minu's enclosure. He murmured so quietly I heard it only because the only other sound was the buzz of nighttime insects.

"Wake up, my lady. What do you say we finally get out this morning for some hunting? The foot looks good. Does it feel all right?" Darius had always struck me as someone of few and blunt words, but there was an ease, a gentle intimacy in his voice as he talked to his roc, as if he whispered to himself. I felt almost intrusive for being there.

Darius gave one short, sharp whistle. Minu flapped through the open doors of the pen with a couple of big, jerky hops, landing on the chariot cadge. She sat calmly while Darius hooded and leashed her. He closed the doors of the pen, first checking that he had everything he needed. He climbed into the chariot and I climbed in beside him. It was just big enough for the two of us and Minu. If I turned, my face was only a breath away from the soft white contour feathers of her breast.

Darius flicked the reins and urged the horses onto the road. We rode in silence through the open country. I had a bothersome feeling I ought to try and make conversation, but Darius didn't seem burdened by the same impulse, so I let the silence sit. It wasn't uncomfortable, the way I thought it would be. We were both glad to be out in the predawn countryside, about to fly a roc. Words seemed unnecessary.

I breathed in deeply and leaned my elbows on the front of the box, watching the stars fade. Darius urged the horses faster; they were pureblood stock from the royal stables, bred to run through the desert with unflagging endurance. The chariot swayed a little under my sandaled feet, rumbling through my soles and up into my legs and body as the wheels ate up the distance. In the east, the sky lightened, then turned pink. The sun rose fast, burning up the wide horizon, spilling its first rays across the dusty scrubland.

The farther we went, the more Darius seemed to relax. His shoulders came down, his movements grew smoother and more assured, the small muscles around his lips and eyes slackened until his expression was almost soft. He eased back on the pace and started scanning. He brought the chariot to a gentle stop at the top of a wide, flat hill. Jumping from the box, he stretched his arms over his head, his long body flexing like a sapling in the wind. I

climbed down after him. We were in a dry, yellow landscape with grassy knolls and dips that hid nests of ground
birds and the dens of burrowing animals.

Darius studied the field with the calculating stare of
an army commander surveying an approach. "We have a
good wind," he murmured approvingly. The strong breeze
at our backs ran into open country, pleasingly devoid of
ravines or heavy cover. Darius would want to flush game
downwind to give Minu the most power possible in her
approach.

"Let's see if we can't find you an easy kill," he said,
untethering his roc. He loosened the braces of her hood
and slipped it off. Minu's sharp eyes seemed to take in the
entire scene at a glance. She roused, fluffing up her feathers. Then she took a crap off the end of the chariot and
launched herself into the air.

I ducked. A bird as large as a roc is not elegant in takeoff or landing. Minu was a maelstrom of feathers and mad
exertion as her massive wings pummeled the air. Darius
had chosen this spot for its higher elevation, which made
it easier for her to get airborne. Minu spread her wings
and rode the downslope of the land, gaining speed, nearly
skimming the ground. She pumped hard, once, twice,
three times, flattening the grass below with the wind, and
caught an air current that lifted her up and away from
us in a straight line. When she was far enough to be a
small silhouette, she curved in a long arc and circled back
toward us. Darius watched her with one hand shielding
his eyes.

I watched too, my heart in my throat at her beauty. Minu was much older than Zahra, glorious in her adult plumage. Her breast was as pure white as a funeral robe; as she sailed through the morning light, the bright tips of her long flight feathers seemed to be licked by fire. She made a long, high circle overhead, waiting and hungry.

I jumped back into the chariot eagerly. Darius jostled my shoulder as he did the same. He said, "Ready?" and without waiting for my answer, he shouted and whipped the reins, sending the horses galloping down the hill.

I hung onto the box as the chariot careened over rough and rocky bits of land, gaining speed. When it hit flat ground, Darius pulled the horses to the right, and then to the left, so we made wide, thunderous zigzags, avoiding shrubs and boulders, the sure-footed horses straining at the bit. Dirt flew. The wind whipped at my hair. Darius yelled, one long jubilant howl, and the laughter that escaped me turned into a wild shout that I added to his.

If anyone saw us, they would think we were reckless youths taking a prized war chariot on a madcap drunken ride that would likely end with our skulls smashed. What we actually were doing was fulfilling our part of the bargain: Minu hunts for us if we bring her to the prey. Our noise and commotion, we hoped, would flush out animals so that Minu, whose eyes can see the toes of a rabbit from high in the sky, would spot quarry.

I grabbed Darius's arm and shouted, "She sees something! She's after it!" but he'd already seen it too, and he pulled the chariot around and stopped. The horses' lathered flanks heaved in and out as we watched. Minu folded her wings in a steep stoop, dropping from the sky. I followed the path of her descent and saw what she was after: a long-legged jackal, loping for cover. It was a large one, tongue hanging out between open jaws, but it was still slighter than a wolf, small prey for Minu. I gripped the chariot box as we start moving again, Darius racing to help, to cut off the jackal's escape.

Minu closed in. She pulled out of her stoop near the ground, wings snapping wide as she leveled out and extended grasping talons. She hit the jackal, but the creature was both fast and clever; at the last second, it leapt nearly straight backward. Minu's feet grazed its rump and tore off part of its tail as the huge raptor barreled past her prey into the dirt. The jackal yipped high with pain and darted, doubling back and running flat out away from the tumbling roc.

We reached Minu a minute later. She was standing on the rocky ground with one foot on the jackal's tail. It looked like a sad, bedraggled trophy, a consolation prize for a botched kill. Minu looked up expectantly at Darius as he hopped down from the chariot and whistled. She jumped back onto the cadge and he gave her a piece of meat from his bag. "You're rusty from being grounded, is all. We're just getting warmed up. Don't you worry, my lady, you'll be back in shape soon." The disappointment was clear in Darius's voice, but he reassured her the way a parent might comfort a child.

Ruhkers train the roc, scout the land, set up the hunt.

But we don't control the outcome; in the end, that is entirely between the hunter and the quarry. That doesn't stop us from feeling responsible. In nature, predators fail to catch their prey far more often than they succeed, but the whole point of the partnership is to improve those odds. I could tell that Darius saw Minu's performance as his own. He chewed his bottom lip, pensive as he hooded and tethered her, no doubt analyzing whether he could have set up the hunt better or gotten there faster to cut off the jackal's escape. He caught my eye for a second as we climbed back into the box but looked away, embarrassed.

Darius angled us west, toward some trees. He wanted to try again, soon, before the sun was too high. We sat under some shade and waited, and within an hour we spotted two vultures circling in the distance. Vultures meant a carcass was near, which also meant whatever was responsible for the carcass was also near. As we started toward the vultures, a group of roe deer emerged from a stand of scrub oak, gliding their way into the open.

It's not a good idea to fly a roc on hoofed animals like deer or boar too often. Wild rocs will go after easier kills at every chance, but we don't want to discourage our birds from going after the big dangerous predators we train them for. Darius hesitated, but I knew what he was thinking and so I said it out loud instead. "I'm sure it would help her confidence."

Darius turned the chariot around and took it to higher ground, behind the trees the deer had come from. We had a nice, strong wind at our backs as we circled the copse and picked up speed in pursuit of the herd. Without a word, Darius handed me the reins and I kept the horses steady as he untethered Minu and pulled off her hood. She launched straight from the moving chariot, barely clearing the heads of the horses and catching the wind as it sped over the treetops.

The deer bolted at the shadow of the enormous raptor. We were running parallel to them now, penning them in on one side, and Minu came at them from the other. There was no time or distance for her to gain the height for a straight dive; instead she pumped hard and sailed into one of the deer at full speed, talons seizing it by the back and slamming it to the ground with an audible *crack*.

When we got there, we saw that the deer's lower half was twisted almost at a right angle to the rest of the body. Minu's blow had broken the deer's spine clean in half. She had torn open the belly with one foot and was already eating. Darius hummed to her and, moving very slowly to show he wasn't trying to steal her kill, he dug around in the carcass and pulled out the deer's heart. "Nicely done, my lady." Minu dipped down and drank from the blood pooled in the chest cavity. When Darius whistled, she hopped back onto the chariot cadge, and he dropped the heart at her feet, then the liver too.

As she ate, we sat and rested, drinking from our canteens. It was past midday. Darius wiped his bloody hands and forearms on the grass, and pulled out a cloth bundle from his bag, inside which he'd wrapped flatbread, some goat cheese, and a handful of figs. Wordlessly, he spread the cloth in front of us and we ate, basking in the sunshine and the satisfaction of his roc's hunt.

When I think of how I met Darius, it's not the instances we initially crossed paths in the mews that come to mind. It's not even those early training sessions with Zahra. It remains that day out in the field with Minu. A person might pass a tree on the path every day and not notice it until it springs fruit at a time they're hungry. I saw Darius clearly for the first time, as a ruhker perfectly in tune with his roc. I wanted that more than anything for myself and Zahra.

After lunch, we set ourselves to field dressing the deer. As we worked, Darius said, "Minu's not the biggest, or the strongest, or the fastest. But she's persistent. She works for every kill." There was affection and admiration in his voice. Minu hadn't been a fledgling when she was paired with Darius. He'd inherited her when she was fourteen years old, already a seasoned veteran, after her previous ruhker died in an accident. Rocs can live for thirty to forty years, so it's not rare for them to outlive their handlers. Despite the fact that rocs are not social creatures, they do get highly attached to routine and, over the years, form a bond with the person who hunts with them and feeds them, making handlers difficult to replace. If Darius hadn't succeeded, Babak would've had to take Minu deep into the mountains and release her.

We hooded and tethered Minu and loaded the deer onto the floor of the chariot. Darius grabbed its front half and I grabbed the back and we swung it up so it was lying right under Minu's cadge, the skinny legs jutting off the back. Darius covered the body with a tarp and weighed the edges down with rocks. We had to step over it to get back into the box. The venison would go to the palace kitchens, where it might even find its way into a dish for the king.

Darius squinted into the distance, steering the chariot toward the vultures we'd seen earlier. We slowed as we approached; if there were wolves or lions feeding, we wanted to have Minu in the air long before they saw us. More vultures had gathered by now, flapping over the dead animal like a feathery black blanket. We didn't have to get close before seeing there was something very wrong.

The carcass lay in the middle of a rutted road. Behind it was an overturned cart, one wheel broken off and lying a short distance away. Bright orange balls lay scattered all around. Darius and I stared for a moment at the strange sight, then he whipped the horses forward in a gallop. The vultures scattered at our intrusion, squawking angrily, their naked heads hunched over their billowing cloak-like bodies. They had been feeding on a dead donkey—recently dead by the looks of it, its head mostly torn off and its eyes pecked out by the carrion birds, but the body not yet bloated or rotten. The colorful balls were tangerines, a whole cartload of them spilled across the dirt.

Where there had been a donkey and a cart, there must've been a person. Instead, we saw scraps of blood-stained light brown fabric and a single man's sandal, lying amid squashed fruit.

The day had been so pleasant up until then that the dark and terrible turn snatched the breath out of my chest. There's only one thing that would kill a man and leave his donkey and possessions to rot on the road. Manticores will eat just about anything when hungry—deer, camels, livestock—but given a choice, they will go after their preferred prey. We are the preferred prey. They hunt where there are small groups of people: roads with travelers, farmed fields and orchards, the outskirts of towns and villages. The farmer would've been on his way to market when the monster glided out from the trees and down to the road. He'd tried futilely to hide behind his donkey.

Thank God he'd been alone.

Darius jumped out of the chariot and walked toward the grisly tableau. He crouched, examining the ground, and touched fingertips to the prints in the dirt, mixed in among the bits of bloody cloth, the mangled donkey, and the sweet, citrus smell of tangerines. He stood. His eyes followed the bloody drag lines in the dirt, leading off the road and into the gully, where they were broken up by the rocky ground. Our eyes lingered on the shadows in the nearby trees, the rocks and grass that might break up the mottled black and tan of a manticore's pelt. The monster was gone by now, but that didn't mean Minu might not see it from the sky.

When Darius came back to the chariot, he put a hand on Minu's jesses, unsure of what to do. Minu had recently recovered from injury, had already hunted twice that day, and had fed just an hour ago. She'd be heavier, slower, and less motivated than she needed to be to tackle a manticore. She could be injured or killed, in which case, Darius and I were dead as well.

But one man wouldn't be enough to satisfy a manticore's appetite. With people nearby, it would kill again as soon as it got an opportunity. The only thing we can rely on to kill a manticore is a roc. Arrows fail to pierce the monster's quilled pelt. Dogs will not face them. In the wild, even wolves and lions avoid them; only the largest bears need not fear. Manticores can't be poisoned and rarely stay in one place long enough to be snared by elaborate traps.

Rocs are their only natural predator, delivering sudden death from the sky in a way nothing can on earth. Perhaps, as the magi say in their stories, ruhking was founded by Raka, the great hero of myth who befriended the Queen of Rocs, but more likely the tradition was born in ancient times by falconers who witnessed wild rocs bringing down prey much larger than themselves, even killing manticores. Moments like this are what we ruhkers train for. Hunting the wolves, lions, and leopards that prey on our livestock is part of our job. Culling deer or wild boar and taking home the meat is a perk. Killing manticores is our duty. Our calling.

Darius steered the horses away from the carnage, following the manticore's drag tracks from the road. When we were far enough away that Minu wouldn't be distracted by the donkey carcass, Darius unleashed and unhooded her. She looked around, then shifted her feet on her perch. For a moment, I thought she was bored or tired and not going to fly, but then she took off, struggling visibly to gain altitude without the advantage of high elevation. Her muscled wings beat in huge, heavy strokes until she hit a good wind current and soared up high over the plain. Darius watched her, worried. I watched for the manticore. If the monster was nearby, all we could do was hope Minu saw it and got to it before it got to us.

The chariot's sturdy wheels navigated the rough terrain. Minu waited overhead, gliding in slow, expectant circles. The drag trail became difficult to follow, but Darius spotted fabric snagged on dry shrubbery beneath a rock outcropping at the base of a hill. It was mingled with bits of white and red gristle. What was left of the unfortunate tangerine farmer looked like it could be tossed out in a pail behind the butcher's for the dogs to bicker over.

There was no path up the hillside and it was too rocky for the wheels to navigate any farther. "I'm going to take a look from up there." Before I could respond, he got out of the chariot and began climbing up the slope in a crouch. I still barely knew Darius; I marveled at his matter-of-fact bravery even as I cursed under my breath and broke into a sweat imagining the manticore rising from the other side of the hill, mouth agape, dragging the man down under its body. To my great relief, he reached the top of the hill safely and straightened up slowly, cautiously. He gazed down the other side of the hill for several minutes, then turned around and came back down, taking hopping steps and skidding a little as he hurried back. "There's a town about two and a half parasangs away," he said. "We need to send word to them."

"Did you see any sign of the manticore?"

Darius shook his head. "Minu hasn't either. It's moved on, or it's hiding and sleeping off its meal." He raised his face to look for his roc. "I'm going to bring her in."

Minu dipped low, close to the chariot, as if questioning what in heaven's fire we were doing standing around and talking—would there be hunting or not? Darius put two fingers to his mouth and whistled so loudly I jumped; clearly he had no need for one of the reed whistles I carried. Minu didn't respond at first. She made another circle, reluctant to land, but on the next pass she came in and hit the chariot cadge, a bit ungracefully. Darius gave her meat from his bag, leashed and hooded her, and took the reins gently from my damp hands. He turned the chariot around and set the horses running for the mews.

It was the right decision; there were only a couple hours of daylight left and Minu wouldn't fly or hunt in the dark. Being out in manticore territory after the sun fell would be a bad idea. Nevertheless, I looked behind us with a cold, helpless ache in my stomach, thinking of the manticore rousing and prowling toward its next meal.

When we got back to the mews, Babak called a briefing. He said we'd done the right thing by hurrying back. By lamplight, we marked the manticore's kill site and direction of travel on one of the large maps that hung in the room. We pointed out the town and circled the nearby areas we thought the manticore might be hiding. The Master of the Mews sent messengers racing out on horseback to warn the townspeople and neighboring farms to arm themselves and shelter in their homes with their doors and windows boarded. At first light he sent three ruhkers and their rocs out to hunt for the man-eating beast.

I waited in suspense for news. Many manticore hunts had taken place since I'd arrived as an apprentice, but this one felt more real and urgent. It was the first attack to occur since I'd gotten Zahra. The day would soon come when my name would be pinned to Babak's map and I would be the one sent out to slay the monster before it could kill again. That day seemed terrifyingly close and still agonizingly far away.

I couldn't stop thinking about the tangerine farmer, wondering what kind of person he'd been, about the family that was now grieving for him yet unable to give his remains a proper cremation. Someone had come to my father's house—it would never again be a home, merely a house—to tell us that the king's ruhkers had caught and killed the monster that ruined my life, but I never knew how much of Arnan and my mother was recovered. I wonder if my father did.

Darius and I learned later that on the night the tangerine farmer was taken, a nearby farm was terrorized. Two field serfs were dragged away and eaten. The family hid in the cellar all night while the manticore tore at their walls before wandering off at dawn. Later that afternoon, one of our ruhkers and his roc tracked down the beast and dispatched it less than a parasang away from the town Darius had spotted from the top of the hill. Thanks to Babak's early warnings, none of the townspeople lost their lives.

I asked Darius if he was disappointed he hadn't been the one to make the kill. Usually the ruhker and roc who flag quarry get the first right to hunt it. Darius shook his head. "Not worth it." Not worth endangering Minu when she wasn't in peak form. As large as a roc is, she still weighs less than a man, while a manticore weighs as much as a bear. Many a tragic hunt has ended with the tables turned, with the manticore injuring or killing the roc, and often a roc will refuse to tackle a manticore if it doesn't feel confident enough. Ruhking is a proud profession that attracts some individuals motivated by personal ego and the number of kills they can attach to their names. Darius wasn't one of those people; he might not be happy about losing his quarry, but he was also relieved not to risk Minu's life.

After that day, the two of us became friends, without ever speaking of it, the way one falls into a comfortable habit. We would arrive at our birds' pens at the same time in the morning, share supplies and chores, watch the other person's roc during training and hunting in the way neighbors in a village watch each other's children. If we'd met outside of the mews under any other circumstance, I doubt we would've been able to keep a single conversation going—Darius was even less naturally sociable than

I was—but a shared obsession with ruhking brought and kept us together as easily as two leaves flowing side by side down the same stream.

~ ⌐

Nasmin returned with three lion skins draped over the front of her chariot, riding up to the mews like a triumphant warrior queen. I was working with Zahra on the training field when I saw her thunder by. What other woman in all of Dartha could travel in the wilderness for ten days, kill three lions, and arrive with a glowing smile and perfect hair, as if making an entrance at a nobleman's banquet?

My moment of envy passed and all I felt was gladness at seeing her back safely.

Nasmin beamed at everyone, even the ones she knew leered or scoffed at her behind her back. She embraced me and kissed my cheeks like a sister. "Come, feel this. Isn't it the softest lion pelt you've ever touched? I think I'll have it made into a rug and sent as a gift to my brother's wife."

Nasmin's enormous rust-colored roc, Azar, stood regal, eyeing everything murderously. She was a fine hunter and tame enough with Nasmin, but liable to take a dislike to other people. I took several steps back just to be safe. Nasmin drew me aside. "I wish I'd been here when your dark days ended," she said apologetically. "I knew you'd be fine, but I still worried and said my prayers five times a day. How's Zahra's training going? When will you be able to take her out?"

"Soon, I think," I told her. Babak had wanted Zahra up in the air within a month, and I was well aware that I was up against his deadline. "She's flying to the wolf lure every time, and back to the cadge on the whistle. I hooded her and took her riding on the chariot for an hour yesterday. She bated from the cadge a couple of times, but settled down quickly."

"I'll come with you on her first free flight," Nasmin promised.

It was strange to be friends with both Nasmin and Darius. They were cordial enough with each other, but so different that when the three of us were together, I felt like a bridge spanning a river between two countries. "Everyone says he's a good ruhker, but he's rather dour and awkward, don't you think?" Nasmin whispered to me. Darius didn't comment on Nasmin, but sometimes after her effervescent personality had passed by us like a summer rain shower, he would sigh in relief, and his hunched shoulders would come down.

Nasmin would come by occasionally while I was working with Zahra and speak with me at length, offering her experience and advice. Darius watched almost all the time but rarely commented. Even their advice on training methods sometimes conflicted. "Cut her weight down further," Nasmin suggested. The hungrier a roc gets, the more eagerly it will hunt. If I fed Zahra less, Nasmin said, I could fly her sooner and start building her confidence

with easy kills. A hungry and confident roc will more re-
liably take on larger prey.

Darius relied less on weight cutting and spent more
time training a roc to the lure and the whistle. In his
opinion it was better to habituate a roc to respond at a
stable weight so it was accustomed to hunting and, more
importantly, returning to the ruhker, even when it was
not famished. Rocs "with fire"—the eagerness to kill—
were motivated, he said, not just by hunger but, like the
ruhker, by the joy of the hunt itself.

I had no idea who was right. So even with all the good
advice, I muddled along, as I suspect all ruhkers do, ad-
justing and doing my best based on what I thought would
work for my bird. Zahra was smart, I was sure of it, but like
parents, a lot of ruhkers think their charges are unusually intelligent. My roc was well-mannered and calmed
quickly even when exposed to new sights and noises. I
never forgot how dangerous she was, but I didn't think
she would maim or kill me intentionally without a good
reason.

But she could be moody, inconstant in her willingness
to do as I asked. Sometimes she responded immediately
to me throwing the lure or blowing the whistle. At other
times, even though I knew she was hungry, she ignored me
or gazed far off into the distance or cleaned her feathers.
Finally, she would glance over with an expression that
seemed to say, "You're still here? Very well, I shall deign to
eat these inadequate scraps you've brought me." It was as
if she wanted to prove to me that everything she did was

still of her own free will and, hungry or not, she would do only what she liked. *Remember, you need me more than I need you.* I imagined that was what she was saying to me in those moments. I didn't need reminding.

Before long, Darius said, "I think she's ready." He tapped an unflagged part of Babak's board. "There's a good, flat stretch of road here. I've taken Minu there before."

Nasmin, Darius, and I rode out on an early summer morning through a countryside strewn with wildflowers beneath a vast unmarred sheet of pale blue sky that stretched from horizon to horizon. Nasmin stood beside me in my chariot and Darius drove his own ahead of ours. There was no laziness or reluctance in Zahra today. When I unhooded her, she sat up straight and tall and swiveled her head back and forth, excited by the incredible expanse of empty yellow land stretching away in all directions. I stepped back to stand beside Nasmin. A gust of wind ruffled my hair and Zahra's feathers, and my heart jumped to my throat as she launched upward.

Her wings pumped—smooth, hard strokes as they plowed the air. The wind carried her off the edge of the embankment and bore her aloft. She was marvelous, and she was flying away from me. My chest clenched like a closing fist and tears pricked the backs of my eyes. I was overcome by Zahra's beauty and the sudden panic that all my work over the past month had been for nothing. I had no hold over her. She was free and leaving me forever.

Nasmin hugged me from behind. "I know," she whispered. "It's terrifying, isn't it?"

Below us, a puff of dust rose up behind clattering wheels as Darius ran his chariot hard down the long, packed-dirt road. Minu was not on it; she was back in the mews. A stuffed wolfskin lure was tied to the cadge with a long rope. It bounced and flew through the dust as the chariot dragged it along at high speed. From this distance, I could envision it was a real wolf, running behind the chariot, pelted by dust until its sleek silver coat was a dirty tan. I held my breath, my eyes sweeping back and forth from the wolf lure to the sight of Zahra rising into the blue. "She's not going after it," I whispered.

"Just wait," Nasmin said.

"She's not, I'm going to lose her."

"Look." Zahra stopped climbing. She seemed to hang in the sky for an eternity of a second, then she banked and curved, swinging around behind the chariot in a great arc. I craned my neck to look up as she soared right over our heads and flattened out into a straight pursuit. Darius flicked the reins to keep the horses running, expertly half-turned in the carriage so he could see Zahra's rapid approach. I didn't dare to breathe.

She chased down the wolf lure and fell upon it, her grasping talons puncturing it, crushing it. Darius kept the chariot horses running, dragging lure and roc along, until he saw Zahra's talons sink into the wolf's head, then he pulled the chariot to a stop.

Nasmin and I whooped and hugged each other, jumping up and down together like silly girls. Then we leapt into my chariot and raced back down the embankment.

When we reached Darius, he was untying the lure while Zahra sat upon it triumphantly. She'd torn it open and was contentedly swallowing the meat I'd stuffed inside earlier. When she'd taken the edge off her hunger, I blew my whistle and held up a fatty piece of camel liver. I dropped it next to her cadge. She cocked her head at me indulgently, made one large hop over the torn wolf-skin, then walked to my chariot, in that comical bobbing way of large birds, but as calm and aloof as could be. She climbed onto the cadge and ate while I tethered her.

Darius wound the rope while I cleaned and patched the lure. Nasmin gushed, talking about Zahra's already impressive wingspan, her beautiful hunting form. She'd be ready for real quarry in no time. There wasn't any awkwardness between Nasmin and Darius; we were all in too good a mood. We traveled a little farther and flew Zahra twice more before the heat began to climb. When we turned back for the mews, I was giddy, unable to stop grinning.

That's how I want to remember the three of us. Not marred and bowed by tragedy, but young and joyous. What I would give to return to those days, riding together across the country on a perfect morning, a roc balanced in the air above us like an angel guarding our happiness.

II

HUNTER

A visitor arrived at the mews. I returned after a day of exercising and training Zahra in the open field to discover an enormous tent had been installed in the clearing behind the men's quarters. A gold and black carriage was parked next to the structure, and four attendants were busying themselves carrying water, unloading supplies, and unharnessing two fine white horses with jeweled bridles.

Prince Khovash, eighth son of the king, had spent two years living in the northeastern mountains of his mother's tribe and had become engrossed with observing wild rocs. Wishing to learn as much as he could about the creatures, he'd come to stay at the Royal Mews to immerse himself in the world of ruhking. "As long as it doesn't interfere with our safety and duties, we're to give him all the deference and obedience afforded his royal station," Babak reminded us.

Various nobles and royals often wished to hunt recreationally and called upon Babak's ruhkers to take them on excursions. The more sensible of these "hunters" were willing to gain their enjoyment from coming along but staying out the way and letting the ruhker and roc do their job. Others insisted on elaborate processions of dozens of horses, hunting dogs, falcons, and, of course, a roc or two. The wealthy nobleman would ride at the front of this ridiculous parade, probably on an elephant or camel. This small army of people and animals would be sent after one poor lion or maybe a pack of wolves.

For the most part, we couldn't say no to these farces, since we were the king's ruhkers after all, and if the request came from the palace, we had to obey. But ruhkers are a proud lot and none of us have any respect for rich, entitled sport hunters. So we all hurried back to our quarters and duties hoping to avoid being called upon to entertain our royal guest.

Being inexperienced, I didn't know that the best way to steer clear of nobles was to not be available in the late morning. During the summer, ruhkers are up well before dawn to fly our birds, returning to the mews in the late morning to bathe and settle our rocs before the heat of midday. That's also around the time rich people wake up and saunter out to begin the day. The morning after the prince and his retinue arrived, the more experienced ruhkers took the morning off flying, or were out and back extra early. I was stupidly the only one in the field behind the mews, filling a bath for Zahra when I saw Babak approaching with an unfamiliar young man in a tooled-leather tunic and red trousers, with a felt cap atop dark, curly hair.

Curses. Seeing no way to escape, I set down my pail of

water and lowered myself to my knees, eyes on the ground as they reached me. "My lord prince," I murmured.

I felt a touch on my shoulder, bidding me to rise. I lifted my gaze tentatively—and struggled not to stare. The face gazing down at me was friendly and curious, softened by a warm, guileless smile I hadn't expected. The only images of royalty I'd ever seen were square-jawed profile portraits of the king. Prince Khovash bore no resemblance to those. His mother had been a princess of the mountain tribes, wedded to Antrius the Bold in tribute, and from her, Khovash had inherited the fair olive complexion of a northerner, made all the more arresting by the ink-black curls of his hair. When he blinked down at my awestruck expression, long lashes brushed the tops of high sculpted cheekbones.

"Is that your roc?" Prince Khovash looked past me eagerly. "What a striking color."

When it appeared that I'd lost the power of speech, Babak cleared his throat pointedly at me and said, "My lord prince, Ester is training one of our newest rocs. This juvenile will gradually lose her immature plumage and darken in color over the next few years." As if acting on a cue to show off for an appreciative audience, Zahra waded into the bath and spread her wings, ruffling them and spraying water over the back of my head and tunic.

"What a divinely magnificent creature," Prince Khovash exclaimed. "What's her name?"

"Zahra, my lord prince." My voice returned alongside a rush of warmth to my head. Hearing a stranger—a handsome prince, no less—praise Zahra so highly made me want to prostrate myself flat on the ground and kiss Prince Khovash's boots to thank him for noticing her magnificence and commenting on it aloud.

"Ester, was it?" Those dark, helplessness-inducing eyes traveled back to me. "I didn't know young women could become ruhkers."

"It's necessary, my lord prince." Babak answered before I could, perhaps to stave off possible criticism. "Some rocs prefer women handlers and do not take well to men. Sometimes the opposite is true. No one but God knows why. So we must always have male and female apprentices."

"It's fitting, though, isn't it? Since only female rocs are flown?" asked the prince.

"Yes, my lord prince," Babak said. "Only the females are large enough to be of use."

Zahra was now hunched in the sun with her wings draped lazily and her eyes closed. She would remain like that for over an hour, without a care in the world. Prince Khovash gazed enthralled. "Tell me, Ester," he said, my name in his mouth rounded and thoughtful, "why did you become a ruhker?"

I glanced at him as if at the sun. "I . . . feel it's what I'm meant to do."

"You believe God put you on earth to fly rocs?" If someone else had said it, the words might've sounded dubious, silly, or scornful. Prince Khovash made them seem right and real.

"Yes, my lord prince." I swallowed. "To fly rocs, and to kill manticores."

Prince Khovash considered this for a long moment. The weight of his assessing gaze felt like a gentle physical pressure, one that tugged on my stomach in an inappropriate way. "Only the best of us," he said with admiration in his voice, "embrace God's purpose as clearly as wild beasts."

No one had ever put it to me like that. Prince Khovash said to Babak cheerfully, "Shall we keep going, then? I'd like to see more of the rocs, though as Master of the Mews you must be very busy, and I don't wish to take up all of your time." Babak grumbled some assurance that showing the prince around was no trouble, and the two of them wandered away.

I think I knelt there for several minutes even after they were gone. Prince Khovash's words that day have lingered with me so long that even now I can't hate him.

⌒‿⌒

Zahra grew sleek and fit. She killed her first jackal so quickly and easily it was almost anticlimactic. Darius was away on a hunt but Nasmin was with me when Zahra took down her first wolf, a lone red male that dove into a stand of scrub oak to evade her. Nasmin flushed it out on horseback, and Zahra hit it with such momentum that she snapped its back and carried it the length of two chariots before landing.

Although I was bursting with pride, I didn't relish killing jackals and wolves. I didn't really want to kill lions either. Zahra had already taken to the lion lure, and I figured it was only a matter of opportunity before she made a kill. I've always loved animals, and when I collected the body of the poor dead wolf, I stroked its blood-matted fur and felt a dull stab of sadness. It was a beautiful creature, and I had ended its life by setting my roc on it. I know it seems contradictory, to love the animals you kill, but a lot of ruhkers feel the same.

Lions and wolves can be hunted by determined humans—they can be killed by archers' arrows or be set upon by dogs. If they were the only predators we had to worry about, there would be no need for ruhking. There's only one reason we follow in the footsteps of the mythical hero Raka, who risked life and limb to make a pact with the queen of the sky.

I began flying Zahra on manticore hide, dragging it behind the chariot on a chain. A manticore pelt is heavy and nearly indestructible. The hairs are layered, densely packed quills that jab you with their tips or make thin, deep cuts across your fingers. I wore thick leather gloves when handling it, but Zahra's impervious scaled talons made short work of the lure. I wondered if the hide I was training her on had belonged to the manticore that had eaten the tangerine farmer and two field serfs earlier that year. When Zahra punched it full of holes, ripped it with her beak, shredded it with her talons, I imagined a real manticore writhing as it was sent violently back to the pit of hell it came from.

In my imagining, the manticore has one brown eye, one blue.

A strange thing happens after a manticore attack. Every day people die from disease or in accidents. Women lose their lives in childbirth, and men in feuds. Far off in the outer reaches of the kingdom, soldiers die in wars against Dartha's enemies. But if five, ten, or fifteen people are killed in a manticore attack, fear grips the surrounding land. People shut themselves in their homes. A prowling monster paralyzes a town, shuts down trade and travel.

An urgent message reached the mews in the middle of the night. A trade caravan from the west on its way to Antopolis had been set upon by two manticores. This was unusual. Manticores are solitary, territorial creatures, but occasionally, the screaming of victims will draw another nearby monster and they will converge on the site of a massacre. Thirteen travelers were devoured. The main eastern road into the capital had been shut down and soldiers were being deployed to protect the area until the man-eaters were found and killed.

Babak assigned three teams to set out at dawn. Darius and I were one of them. I knew as soon as Babak looked at me that he wanted to see Zahra prove herself. I'd taken

my time training her, and he was satisfied with her progress. She'd taken down jackals and wolves and one lion.
Now it was time to see if she had what it took. If she was
a manticore killer.

I barely slept that night and rose to dress in the dark
while praying to God the supreme Fire Bringer to grant us
success. Earlier, I'd dragged the manticore pelt into Zahra's
pen and left it on top of a hunk of camel liver that the
butcher had saved for me. I didn't know if it would put her
in the mood to go after manticore today, but it couldn't
hurt. When I returned to the pen, I saw that the pelt had
been torn in half and crapped on. I took that as a good
sign.

Darius didn't look any different than he normally did
as he loaded up supplies and opened Minu's pen. Then
again, Darius never looked much different. It was hard
to tell if he was anywhere as nervous as I was, but he was
talking to Minu a lot in that soothing low voice he used
only with her.

With the road so empty, and our horses swift and fresh,
we reached the site of the attack in less than an hour.
Soldiers had marked a perimeter around a section of road
that looked as if it had been hit by a windstorm. One
covered wagon was still standing, but three others were
on their sides. Two of them were smashed nearly to splin-
ters. Horses lay dead on the road, still tangled in their
harnesses. Objects were scattered all about: bolts of fine
silk, metal pots and pans, broken ceramic, chairs, musical
instruments, even children's toys. Soldiers were righting

the wagons, gathering the scattered goods, and loading them back into the vehicles that were still serviceable. The ground was covered with dark, sticky patches that had sunken into the dirt and stained the grass, and the bloody footprints of the soldiers' boots crisscrossed the scene. Two sad-looking dogs wandered about. One of them stopped every once in a while to whine mournfully; the other licked at the blood on the ground.

One of the soldiers motioned us to a halt and approached with torch held aloft. "What's this?" Darius demanded, staring at all the activity, aghast. "Your men have tromped all over and made a mess." If we'd seen the area before the soldiers walked over it, we could've discerned prints, drag marks, blood trails, to determine how large the monsters were and in which direction they'd traveled.

The captain sniffed angrily. "You want us to leave bodies lying in plain view? Tempt thieves with all this lying around? Our orders are to clean this up and get the road reopened. You do your jobs and let us do ours." He eyed Minu and Zahra with fearful fascination. "Don't let those creatures near our horses. They're jumpy enough with the stink of manticore all over the place."

We examined the area anyway, and Darius was able to surmise that there were indeed two sets of manticore prints, one slightly bigger than the other, each leading away from the scene in a different direction. When Nasmin and Sami arrived a few minutes later, they decided to chase the larger manticore north. Darius and I would track the smaller one eastward, back down the road and into the rising sun, which was tinting the landscape a pale yellow as it climbed over the trees.

We drove slowly, on the lookout for blood, fur, prints, tattered clothes. Every once in a while we stopped and got down to search more carefully on foot. I spotted scraps of fabric clinging to shrubbery and Darius found a flattened patch of grass with fragments of human bone where the monster had stopped to gnaw on a femur it had carried away. The blood was dark and dried, hours old. The ordinarily well-traveled road was eerily deserted, and by now we'd been on it for hours. I hadn't eaten anything since yesterday and, despite my nerves, my stomach was tight with hunger. The hunt was urgent, but we still needed to pause to rest ourselves and the horses.

"What was your first manticore kill?" I asked Darius as we passed bread and dates and waterskins to each other.

He rubbed the back of his neck and gazed into the distance, scanning, always scanning. "My first kill with Minu was a couple of years before you arrived at the mews. It was a small female we spotted in the brush while we were alone, hunting lion. Small for a manticore, that is."

"Were you scared?"

He frowned slightly, as if trying to recall exactly how he'd felt that day. "Yes," he said. "But I trusted Minu would know what to do. So I loosed her, and I rode down to where the manticore was and baited it into the open. When it came for me, I raced it and didn't look back. I could hear it, though." A slight shudder ran across his shoulders. "I thought I was going to die."

My stomach performed a small acrobatic maneuver at the thought of being chased down by a manticore and falling under its claws and teeth. At times, the only way for a ruhker to draw a monster into the open is by offering themselves as bait. It's the most terrifying part of the life we've chosen. In those moments, the ruhker's life is entirely dependent on their roc and whether she reaches her quarry before the manticore does.

Darius gazed at me, no doubt reading my anxious thoughts. "Zahra will know what to do. Just like Minu did." The calm surety in his voice made me look up at him. With Darius, I never felt the need to fill silence, but when our eyes met, I thought I ought to say something, to thank him for being a balm to my confidence.

Minu shifted her feet impatiently. Zahra appeared to be asleep, but Minu bobbed her hooded head and picked at the jesses with her beak, then opened her wings and flapped them, as if she might bate off the cadge. Darius spoke to her apologetically and got us moving again.

We hadn't gone far before a puff of dust rose on the road behind us. I put a hand over my eyes and squinted to make it out. A messenger was racing toward us. When he drew near, the apprentice reined in his horse and jumped to the ground. "Nasmin and Sami caught the other manticore," he panted excitedly as he ran up. "It was traveling slowly, carrying away a body. Azar spotted it and killed it before it could run."

I was relieved the monster was dead, and I was delighted for Nasmin to have added such a dramatic kill to

Azar's hunting record. I would be running to congratulate her when this was over. But the pressure was squarely on me and Darius now, to catch the second manticore before it could elude us and kill again.

We continued our hunt with grimmer determination. This manticore was moving quickly, unencumbered by victims. Fortunately, a beast as large as a manticore doesn't slip away easily. I spotted it first, an hour later. Initially a glimpse, easily mistaken for moving shadows, a mottled shape distantly shifting in and out of view behind a line of trees. My heart rose into my throat as I stopped the chariot, unsure if my wishful eyes were lying to me. They weren't, and I didn't need to say a thing; Darius saw it as soon as I pointed.

We leapt to untether our rocs. Zahra was awake now and ready to fly, but Minu was shuffling on the cadge, ruffling her feathers and shaking her head as if trying to dislodge her hood.

We looked between our birds. It was obvious Minu wanted to hunt. But this was Zahra's chance. My chance. Our first real opportunity to kill a manticore. If we succeeded, I would be a real ruhker at last. I would travel to Antopolis to be blessed with holy ash by the magi in the Fire Temple. I would trade the apprentice's yellow tunic for the red and brown of a hunter with full status in the Royal Mews. Who knew when my next chance might arise?

I hadn't known Darius for long, but I knew what he

would do if our positions were reversed. I bit my lip. "Fly Minu," I said.

Darius hesitated. It meant a lot, that considerate second of doubt. "Are you sure?"

"There will always be another manticore," I insisted. "It's more important we bring this one down before it can kill again. Minu has more fire in her right now."

Darius didn't argue. He went to his roc. "Still, my lady," he murmured. Minu heard him approaching and quieted. As soon as he unhooded her, she rocked the back wheels of the chariot as she launched off the cadge, massive wings pumping until she caught an updraft and rose quickly into the sky.

"I'll be faster on horseback." Darius motioned our accompanying apprentice off his horse and swung himself into the saddle. He tightened his belt, cinching his akinaka closer to his body.

I was filled with sudden terror for him. I opened my mouth to tell him to be careful, or something equally nonsensical, but before I could get out a single word, he wheeled the horse around and galloped for the trees. My face was frozen as I watched him race toward the manticore. Minu was high overhead now, and even though I knew her raptor's eyes could see Darius as clearly as I could, she seemed too far away to help. I'd lost sight of the monster by now; it had vanished into the landscape. But I knew it was there.

Darius screamed. I nearly jumped out of my skin. Darius

was so quiet, so unobtrusive in every way that the sound of him howling was shocking. Even from a distance, the cry carried clearly, and it was convincing. A prey noise, irresistible to the man-eater.

A huge mottled shape burst from the trees and bounded straight for Darius.

My heart threatened to hurl itself clear from my chest. Darius hung on as his mount swerved and fled from the monster, eyes rolling as it put on a burst of frightened speed. The manticore gave chase, its long feline limbs eating up the distance. I was stunned by the sight of the hideous reaper, how silent and graceful it was. Death itself closing in.

I jerked my eyes up in time to see Minu spiral into a straight stoop, plummeting fast toward the ground. My breath caught. At that speed, that height, how could she judge her direction precisely enough? It would be like an archer shooting a moving target while falling from the top of a mountain—surely, a one in a million chance.

I was going to have to watch Darius die.

Minu slammed into the manticore, smashing her weight into its shoulder. Both creatures went to the ground in a somersaulting blur, the manticore flipping over its own head. I sucked in a breath, readying a shriek of triumph, but the manticore rose again, like a heaving wave, and then all I could see was a mass of violent motion—feathers, quills, flapping wings and grasping talons, and the manticore's spiked tail whipping around viciously like the head of a venomous snake. Its apelike face was a snarl of fear and wrath. It twisted violently, spastically, and tore free of Minu, leaving her clutching a hunk of its pelt in her talons. The monster scrambled to its feet and ran.

Darius raced to where his roc sat on the ground, panting with her beak open. He swiveled in his saddle to wave both his arms at me. "Zahra!" he bellowed. "Let her go, now!"

A stab of physical panic, as if I'd been slapped awake in the middle of a falling nightmare, had me moving before I could think. I jumped into the chariot, my hands shaking. "Fly, Zahra, please." I untethered her and pulled off her hood.

Zahra perked up and blinked, taking in the entire scene in an instant. Everything was new to her. She had never seen this place nor a live manticore. She fixed her eyes on the fleeing monster, yet didn't move, and my chest seized with panic. What if she wouldn't fly? What if she didn't know what to do?

With the suddenness of a rock launched from a slingshot, Zahra leapt off the cadge and soared at the fleeing manticore in a straight chase. Her quarry was injured and stumbling fast for the trees. Zahra didn't slow. She was the tip of a thrust spear, traveling in a single unstoppable line. She struck the head of the fleeing manticore with open talons, crushing its skull, dropping it beneath her at once.

When I reached her in the chariot, she was a frightful and marvelous sight, standing on top of the manticore's bulk, her talons buried in its face, her beak glistening with bits of gore. Her crop was already bulging with meat. I was afraid to approach, certain I was disturbing some primal interaction humans had no right to be a part of. Zahra turned her unblinking amber gaze on me, and I felt as I did that first day she was brought to the mews: awed, frightened, unable to believe I could hold such a creature. Her sheer physicality seemed otherworldly, something that puny humans could not lay claim to. When my whistles and camel-liver offerings coaxed her back onto the cadge, my hands shook with relief as I tethered her.

Darius arrived with Minu back on her cadge and hooded. My friend jumped down from his chariot without a word, pulling on heavy gloves and taking his skinning knives straight to the manticore's corpse. "This was just as much Minu's kill," I said quickly. "I hope you don't think any less of how she did just because Zahra finished the job."

Darius paused with the skinning knife poised over the monster's belly, judging where to make the first cut. "I would never think less of Minu." He glanced over his shoulder at me. A small smile pushed up the soft corners of his mouth. "But I'm proud of Zahra. She's a manticore killer now."

Only then did I understand that he hadn't doubted me or Zahra for a second. I'd imagined he was upset, but he was simply treating me as a fellow ruhker, getting down to the task of field dressing as if we were old hunting partners. His matter-of-fact attitude was greater praise than any words. I picked up my skinning knife and got to work.

Dead, the manticore was just like any other game. It was far too large to transport whole, so we would have to skin and dismember it before loading it onto our chariots. The pelt would be turned into lures or mounted, the meat would go to our rocs. It's hard work to field dress a manticore. The quills would've lacerated our hands if we hadn't had thick gloves, and the tough hide could only be sawed through at certain places on the monster's underside and behind its joints. Even with sharp knives and both Darius and me working, it took a long time, with the vultures circling over us and the sun baking down on our heads. When we got through to the organs, Darius fed them to Minu. She certainly deserved them. We moved our rocs into the shade some distance away, where they could sleep off their meals.

The messenger had taken his horse and ridden off to spread the good news that the second manticore was dead. Darius and I had gutted and turned the massive carcass over to drain, and were thirstily guzzling from our waterskins before tackling the big job of skinning, when a handful of riders came galloping toward us. I raised my head to them, my hair plastered to my face with dirt and sweat and my arms covered in gore past my elbows, and there was Prince Khovash, shining and pristine, sitting astride a pure white stallion, surrounded by his royal attendants and staring down at me and the mess of a half-butchered manticore with his full lips parted in astonishment.

I blinked stupidly for a moment before dropping hastily to my knees and tugging Darius down beside me. "My lord prince," we mumbled.

Prince Khovash got off his horse and walked past us toward the dead monster. His retinue dismounted and followed tentatively behind him, gawking. The prince bent over the steaming mass of the manticore's innards, lying in a whitish pile next to the body. He shuddered and stepped away, no doubt realizing that the bulging stomach sac contained half-digested human flesh.

Despite my equal horror at the thought, I couldn't help smiling wryly as I kept my head bowed. It was good for these nobles from the city to see the monster's body. It showed them manticores weren't supernatural. They weren't invincible. They were monstrous animals, but they were still animals. They could be hunted and killed, the way they hunted and killed us.

"You slew this demon?" Khovash asked. "The two of you and your rocs?"

To my surprise, Darius spoke. "It was Ester and Zahra's first manticore kill, lord prince."

Prince Khovash laughed. It was the most delighted laugh I'd ever heard from a grown man. To my abject amazement and self-conscious mortification, he pulled me and Darius to our feet and clapped a hand to each of our shoulders, dirtying his royal person and his fine clothes.

"Almighty Fire Bringer!" the prince exclaimed. "My

good ruhkers, you are like Raka himself, commanding rocs out of the sky! Heroes of Dartha should not kneel."

⌒⌒

Zahra was a manticore killer.

I was a manticore killer.

I would come to a halt at random times during the day— while eating or dressing, walking to and from the mews, sweeping mutes from Zahra's pen—to stare in a trance at nothing.

I could not have felt more bathed with purpose if a column of holy flame had erupted before me with the thundering voice of God. My desire to be a ruhker had been my sole ambition for years, and now I could barely grasp the reality of having achieved it. I was giddy and a little lost, unsettled, burning with impatience to hunt again yet irrationally afraid to do so, lest the first success had been a fluke.

Is a manticore's evil appetite born when it first tastes human flesh? In that moment, does it bask in a rush of epiphanic joy, knowing what it is? If so, perhaps we ruhkers have something in common with our enemy. I understood the monster's insatiable urges better than I could've ever imagined. Having had one taste, I only desired more. With that first kill, I would never again be the terrified girl at the bottom of the well. Ahead of me stretched a shining road stacked with the pelts of demons.

I traveled to Antopolis with Nasmin, not standing in a

chariot as I was accustomed to, but reclining in a pillowed
carriage with hanging silks to shield us from the midday
sun. A pair of horses pulled Zahra's crate along behind
us. I kept glancing out anxiously, worried my roc was unhappy to be back in the box that had first taken her from
the nest to the mews. I wished the day's journey to be over
quickly. Nasmin pressed my hand, her smile wide and re-
laxed as she urged me to enjoy our trip. "You'll only get
your ashes once, after all," she reminded me. I was glad to
have her with me; Nasmin's family was from Antopolis,
and this was an ordinary, unfrightening trip for her.

Prince Khovash had returned to the capital, but his
enthusiasm for ruhking had only grown during his stay
at the mews and from witnessing the successful manticore hunt. Khovash longed to be a ruhker himself, but
as his life was too valuable and his social obligations too
numerous, the next two fledglings to be brought into the
mews would be named in his honor and he would help to
choose the apprentices who would train and fly them. At
the prince's request, Nasmin and I were to be recognized
during a feast at the royal court. I would've had to journey
to Antopolis with Zahra in any case, but it was thanks to
Prince Khovash that I traveled in such opulent comfort
and with Nasmin instead of Babak.

The thought of Prince Khovash asking for me by name
sent a warm flush prickling through my body and distracted
me enough that I forgot my impatience to reach the city.
I knew I was being foolish to imagine a prince taking any
special interest in me. Yet I couldn't help thinking of the

way his eyes had rested on my face that first day he'd arrived at the mews. I was a commoner, but he'd smiled at
me with such joy after Zahra's first manticore kill, calling
me a hero of Dartha. Prince Khovash was surely unlike
other nobles; he esteemed people not simply for their station, but for what they could *do*, and most importantly,
for what their *rocs* could do. So we had something vital in
common despite our great difference in status.

We clattered into Antopolis before nightfall. I pulled
back the carriage silks as we passed through the enormous
wooden gates flanked by giant, roc-headed stone guardian
statues, towering six times higher than an ordinary man.
I marveled, open-mouthed, at the city's paved streets, the
crowded markets swarming with people in brightly colored tunics and robes, the gleaming white interior walls
of the city carved with sprawling relief images of Dartha's
grand history and the deeds of its kings and warriors. Antopolis filled my nostrils with the pungent smells of spices
in open baskets, camels being led along by merchants,
sweat and perfume, incense, and unwashed bodies. It
was a wondrous riot of disordered human energy, far too
much for a simple country naïf like me to take in all at
once. My heart thudded, bright and fearful with anticipa-
tion. I'd never felt so out of place.

"Isn't it wonderful?" Nasmin smiled at my awestruck
gaping.

We were fed and lodged in a luxurious inn not far from
the royal palace. Attendants carried hot water for our
baths, scented with rose oil. Our room had the softest

linen sheets I'd ever felt, with hanging curtains over a carved wooden headrest. Dinner was a lamb and eggplant stew spiced with cinnamon and saffron, served with fresh bread and peppermint tea. I kept thinking I couldn't afford such extravagance, then remembering I didn't have to, as it was being paid for out of the royal purse.

Zahra's crate was placed next to the stables. When I went out to check on her, two stablehands, a passing merchant and his young son, and the innkeeper all came over to watch. As I brought Zahra into the stable yard to feed her, they stood around, shuffling back and forth nervously, caught like sparrows in a crosswind between magnetic fascination and natural fear.

"Are you really one of the king's ruhkers?" called the merchant's son, a boy of no more than eight or nine years. When I said I was, his round eyes widened with admiration and he clutched his father's sleeve.

I smiled at the boy with indulgent pride. Manticores were a danger on the farms and roads, the wide-open parts of the country, and the outer reaches of the kingdom. These city folk knew little to nothing of the monsters that roamed beyond their gates. They encountered rocs only in the form of distant sightings, songs and stories, decorative carvings and royal crests. Yet they heard enough to understand that being a ruhker was a difficult and unusual achievement, not something any ordinary person could do.

I fed Zahra a large meal, nearly half a goat, so the next

morning, she was sleepy and placid in the outdoor rotunda of the Fire Temple. We stood before the eternal flame, encircled by stone columns of dazzling white. A dour old magus smeared holy ash across my forehead and dusted it over Zahra's back and wings, blessing us and our partnership in service of God and king.

As he finished speaking, the sun broke through a patch of cloud, Zahra roused, and sacred white ash billowed all around us in a corona of divinely powdery light. I felt as if my soul floated in the dust.

For one cruel moment, I wished my father was there to see me happy.

I spent the afternoon uncharacteristically fretting over my appearance, yanking at my hair with an ivory comb, wondering how much makeup to wear (none and I would look like a little girl, too much would make me appear to be a married woman), trying to apply kohl to my eyes and powder to my face and moaning in dismay at the amateurish results.

At last Nasmin swept into the room and rescued me, taking the brush from my hand and saying, "Oh, Ester, let me do that." I was embarrassed to need her help and so grateful for it that I nearly burst into tears. The high emotions I'd been riding for the past week were running out like the last bit of wool off a spindle. Only the ridiculous thought that the prince might notice and be disappointed by my absence prevented me from throwing myself onto the bed and sulking there for the rest of the night.

I wished to have Nasmin's cheerful social ease, or else to be as self-contained as Darius. He deserved to be recognized at court as much as I did; Zahra might not have brought down the manticore at all if Minu hadn't injured it first. But when I suggested to him that perhaps Babak could request a third invitation to court, Darius had reacted with horror.

"Stuffing myself into robes and trying to make polite talk with nobles who know nothing of ruhking but will pretend they do in order to ask inane questions?" Darius shuddered. "Holy fires, no." He wasn't at all unhappy to stay in the mews. At the moment, I wished I'd made the same choice, but if I had, I would've been miserable, loathing myself for not being brave enough to go to the feast.

Thanks to Nasmin, I was presentable and much calmer by the time we arrived at the palace garden an hour later. Prince Khovash greeted us as if we were his childhood friends, throwing his arms wide with welcome. "Nasmin! Ester! I'm glad I could separate you from your rocs for long enough to give you even a bit of the public honor you deserve."

The prince's pleated red robes were patterned with white blossoms, his dark hair and beard were curled in perfect tight ringlets, and black kohl accentuated the size and intensity of his luminous eyes. He shone like chariot gold, like the morning sun over scrubland, like the bronze of Zahra's wings. Nasmin and I dipped to our knees, fabric pooling around us, and kissed his hands. I was accustomed to wearing functional clothes for hunting and working in the mews: loose men's trousers, tunic, and boots. The beautiful white robe I'd borrowed from Nasmin was gathered up under a wide golden belt to fit my shorter stature, but I still felt as if I were drowning in fabric and unsure of how to move properly.

"My lord prince," we murmured in unison. Nasmin added, "The kingdom is blessed to have a royal son who so deeply appreciates rocs and their divine purpose." Her face remained lowered, but her long lashes flitted as she raised her eyes. She was wearing a rich purple chiton and a short cape of the softest squirrel skin. Her hair, normally tightly coiled under a hunting cap, hung in a long single plait over one shoulder all the way down to her waist. "If all nobles understood and supported our purpose as well as you, there would be far fewer manticores in your father's realm."

I flushed and wished that I'd thought to say something equally eloquent and insightful before the prince. Smiling, Khovash touched our shoulders to bid us rise. "It's my precise hope that your presence here tonight will be an inspiration. Come, let me introduce you to General Zubin."

General Zubin was a tall, barrel-chested man wearing a lion-skin cloak and an embroidered fillet over a stern brow. He walked with the slightly swaying bowleggedness of a man who spent his life in the saddle. "Prince Khovash hasn't been able to stop talking about you ruhkers and your birds." The general looked down his long aquiline nose at us. "I knew there were women ruhkers," he said, "but I wouldn't think that beautiful young ladies need choose such harsh lives over home and family."

"They do so for the safety of Dartha," Prince Khovash said proudly.

General Zubin plucked a cluster of grapes off a serving tray held up to us by one of the passing palace slaves. "Yes, well, if only manticores could be cowed by female beauty, I would send a thousand maidens to fight in the east," he grumbled. "The farther we expand our borders, the more of these monsters we encounter. It's the work of the Deceiver. He's angered at the kingdom's prosperity and so he sends underworld servants to strike fear into our hearts. More attacks occur on villages each year."

This grim news put a damper on the triumph I'd felt in the Fire Temple that morning. We ruhkers toiled every day and traveled wherever we were called. We risked our lives and the lives of our rocs. There were outposts of the Royal Mews throughout the realm, with hundreds of ruhkers dedicated to keeping the land safe. Yet General Zubin was saying that it still wasn't enough. I'd been so proud of Zahra's first manticore kill. Yet how many more monsters were prowling the borderlands of Dartha tonight, snatching children up in razored jaws while we drank and feasted?

I didn't have time to dwell on that morbid thought;

a covered litter draped with red velvet arrived, borne on the shoulders of six men. Antrius the Bold and two of his wives emerged from behind the curtains of finery and took their places at the royal table. In person, the monarch was shorter than I'd expected, more friendly in appearance than his unsmiling, straight-jawed likenesses depicted on gold coins and the sides of imperial buildings. Ornate robes layered him in red, gold, and white, representing the eternal flame, and his jeweled diadem bore the royal crest of the one-eyed roc, representing the unified authority of God and monarch.

Prince Khovash approached the high-backed chair and knelt to kiss his father's hand. The king squinted at him for a long enough moment that I wondered if he was trying to remember the prince's name. Antrius the Bold had twelve sons, after all. "Khovash," he said at last. "Returned from another far-flung patch of wilderness, I see. What a surprise to see you in court and in clean clothes."

The courtiers tittered, but they did so affectionately. Handsome, warm-hearted Prince Khovash seemed to be well liked. Perhaps the fact that he was eighth in line to the throne meant he had few political ambitions and no enemies and was allowed to devote all his time to indulging his personal interests.

Khovash rose to his feet and smiled, unoffended by the lighthearted amusement at his expense. "Father, may I present for your recognition two of your loyal subjects, ruhkers of the Royal Mews."

Nasmin and I stepped forward and prostrated ourselves.

My hands were clammy and I was glad I didn't have to say anything, as Khovash spoke on our behalf, not only to the king but to the entire gathering of royalty and nobles. "No more than ten parasangs from the gates of the city, two manticores attacked a caravan bound for Antopolis. They massacred the travelers and surely would've gone on to devour many more innocent souls had they not been heroically slain by trained rocs directed by the will of these courageous maiden warriors you see before you."

I didn't look up, but I could feel the king's gaze resting curiously on our bowed heads. "Your commendable deeds serve and glorify the realm. You are welcome guests." His voice resonated with authority, smooth as the surface of a winter lake. We shuffled forward to kiss the back of his hands—they were cool and papery—before he waved us off with a gesture of benevolent blessing and dismissal. As we backed away, other courtiers came forward to seek a personal audience with the king, but I don't remember any of them. Nasmin was glowing, smiling beatifically, but I was relieved simply to have gotten through it.

The rest of the evening passed as if in a bright dream. There were more people to talk to—a rotation of strangers in expensive clothes and powdered faces whose multitudinous names and titles I couldn't hope to hold in my head, all asking me a battery of eager questions about rocs and ruhking. At first, I stammered with nervousness, but then I remembered I was an expert in a subject dear to my heart, and the thought allowed me to relax. It was easy to talk about ruhking, and a goblet of wine in my hand made it easier. Soon, I found myself enjoying the attention, the validating nods of admiration from people of such great wealth and high status. I was glad I'd come after all. Nasmin was right; Antopolis was splendid, and I owed it all to Zahra. She had brought me, a farmer's daughter from a small satrapy in the south, all the way to the shining palace of the king.

Servants brought out food, more than I'd ever seen in my life: platters of smoked fish and grilled lamb; rich stews of vegetables and beans seasoned with onions and herbs; plates of olives and dates; buttery rice with nuts and saffron; sweet pastries with almonds and pistachios. An endless supply of wine flowed into goblets. Lamps were lit, casting dancing firelight shadows onto laughing faces as the sun set behind the palace walls. I wasn't accustomed to so much food and wine and human interaction, and my gauzy sense of happiness was muddled with exhaustion and jitteriness. The king had left, which meant the guests were permitted to drift away from the feast as well. I turned to look for Nasmin, hoping she'd agree it was time we returned to our room in the inn. I still needed to check on Zahra before I collapsed into bed.

Nasmin wasn't where she'd been a few minutes ago. I stood up on my toes, trying to see over the heads of the people nearby. "Are you looking for your friend?" Two young women, daughters of some nobleman, giggled and pointed to the gardens.

I made my way through the thinning clusters of socialites and past a line of perfectly ordered palm trees standing sentinel along a broad stone walkway. The rising moon was frayed by a quilt of torn clouds, its light silvering the long reflecting pools. At the center of the garden was a square fountain, water bubbling gently over rocks. Beside the fountain, Nasmin stood with Prince Khovash, their voices low in conversation, their heads bent close together like those of courting swans. The prince took Nasmin's hand and pressed it passionately to his chest, then bent to kiss her. Their lips met and the outlines of their silhouettes came together.

I backed away without a sound. Returning to the palace courtyard, I milled aimlessly with the few remaining guests, picking at the platter of sad leftover olives, not because I had any appetite, only to give myself something to do, anything at all to look as if I was still enjoying myself. I wished we were close enough to the inn that I could walk back alone. I felt like a mountainous fool.

A few minutes later, Nasmin returned, smiling freshly, as if we hadn't been at the party for hours. "Ester, there you are!" Seeing my expression, she asked, "What's wrong?"

"Nothing," I said. "I'm exhausted, that's all."

It mortifies me now to think of how obvious my resentment must've been. Nasmin waited until we were alone in the carriage on the way back to the inn before turning to me with a serious expression that didn't dampen the flush in her cheeks. "Tonight wasn't just an evening to dress up and enjoy ourselves, Ester. It was an opportunity. Do you remember what I said about how the Royal Mews ought to have more support? Prince Khovash took that to heart. He wants to do whatever he can to help."

I did her the favor of appearing intrigued, interested, ready to be happy. "And?"

Nasmin smiled at me as winningly as ever, her teeth a glimmer of white in the dark, but she didn't seize my hand warmly the way she usually did. Already, I sensed something forming between us, tendrils of guilt and envy weaving like fast-growing vines into the cracks of our friendship. Nasmin wanted to share her achievement, and she couldn't do so without hurting me. We had both come to Antopolis as celebrated ruhkers, but only one of us was leaving a hero.

"Prince Khovash wants to embark on a royal tour to promote ruhking across all of Dartha," she told me. "He's asked for me and Azar to travel with him as ambassadors, to show nobles and common folk alike who've never seen rocs up close just how splendid they are and how they keep the realm safe. He believes that Azar and I will inspire people to become apprentices, and we'll be able to collect taxes and donations that'll go toward supporting the Royal Mews." She took my hand at last, but there was a quickness to it that felt like a plea for understanding. "It could be a great help to all of us, Ester."

"Nasmin, that's wonderful!" I think I sounded sincere in the moment. At least I wasn't petty enough to mention the kiss, to point out that she was to be the chosen ambassador for the Royal Mews because the prince was as enamored with *her* as he was with rocs. Learning that Nasmin and Khovash hadn't snuck off to the garden simply as smitten lovers, but to have a discussion about ruhking somehow made me feel worse, even more like a trampled-over weed. All I wanted in that moment was to get back to Zahra, back home to the mews where I had worth.

"If the tour goes well, perhaps there will be more in the future, and we could travel together," Nasmin pointed out with bright, overly considerate optimism.

"Oh no," I said quickly. "Tonight was more than enough socializing with nobility for me. I can't wait to get out of these robes and back to hunting, even if the food in the mews won't ever taste as good after this." We laughed together. "I'll miss you when you're gone, though."

That was truer than I could've imagined even then.

III

CAPTOR

My life in the Royal Mews changed. It wasn't that Babak treated me any differently. He didn't care that I'd been feted in Antopolis and presented before the king. When I returned from the trip, he glowered at me and grumbled terse commands as he always did, interrogated me about Zahra's weight, told me I'd have to pick up double shifts cleaning the roc pens to make up for my absence.

I was a little stung by Babak's dismissiveness, but I later came to understand that it came from the cynicism of experience. The true worth of a ruhker was in long days of hunting and uncelebrated toil. The first manticore kill, receiving holy ashes in the Fire Temple, the royal feast where I was made to feel special—they would never happen again. Babak was simply reminding me of that, giving me ashes in his own way.

What was different was the way the other ruhkers spoke to me. As most apprentices don't last more than a year or two, experienced ruhkers pay them little mind. Now that Zahra and I had proven ourselves, however, the older men and women whose shadows I used to skirt behind, who I would hurriedly step aside for on the path as they walked past me without so much as a glance, greeted me by name in the dining hall, asked questions about Zahra's progress as a hunter, shared with me their knowledge and the meat from their roc's kills. I went from having only two real friends to being accepted by an entire community.

Getting to know so many veteran ruhkers only fueled my obsession. I would wait for Babak outside of the map room before dawn, hoping to be the first to pin my colored flag to the board and claim a preferred hunting area. I went out with Darius as often as I could, but I began hunting with some of the other ruhkers as well, the ones who didn't mind having a less experienced partner along. I put Prince Khovash and Nasmin out of my mind and threw myself into work.

The second manticore Zahra killed was a juvenile male that had been sighted stalking along a road but had fortunately not eaten anyone yet. It was likely new to the area. I climbed into the low branches of a broad cypress tree and yelled myself hoarse for fifteen minutes while Zahra floated above, her immense size reduced to a silhouette that I could cover by closing one eye and holding my thumb up to the sky. The monster came prowling hesitantly but hungrily through the grass, only the mottled hump of its back visible, its demonic ape face low to the ground. My chariot horses, tethered to the tree, tossed their heads and stamped, their eyes rolling with fear. The sight of the monster's approach stole the last bit of moisture from my raw throat and made my blood run to ice.

Darius waited with Minu at a distance, ready to charge in and help if need be, but no help was needed. Zahra fell in a breathtaking stoop, silent and deadly as a spear hurled from heaven, striking the manticore near the base of its head. The impact of the monsters flattened the grass and earth around them. The manticore let out a bloodcurdling noise, a sound I'd never heard before and wouldn't want to hear again—a shriek far too horribly childlike. It had been a newish demon, one that hadn't yet left a long trail of human victims, and Zahra had snuffed it out.

I scrambled out of the tree, scraping my hands and knees, and leapt into the chariot. Darius reached the scene before I did, but when he didn't even draw his akinaka, I knew the job was done. Zahra was eating out of the monster's crushed skull. I was as proud of her as I had been the first time, but this time, there would be no trip to the Fire Temple, no blessings or feast. From now on, our satisfaction would be expected and workmanlike.

"Slaying one manticore is impressive to most people," Darius reminded me as we struggled, panting and sweating, to hook the carcass to the back of my chariot, "but it's easy compared to doing this over and over again."

Darius was right; Zahra and I had only just begun. But with that second success, we were on our way to being like Darius and Minu and the other senior ruhkers and their rocs—able to kill routinely, habitually, professionally.

Nasmin's grand tour of the realm with Prince Khovash lasted for three months and was a great success, as I'd expected it would be. Nasmin was a perfect spokesperson to the royal court and the common people alike. She rode into towns seated in a gilded carriage next to Prince Khovash, fearsome Azar perched behind them. She recounted the stories of brave Raka meeting the Queen of Rocs to wide-eyed children; she flew Azar to the lure in demonstrations for awed villagers; she shared her captivating personal journey from being the middle daughter of a merchant family in Antopolis to an apprentice in the mews, the only one that mercurial Azar would accept as a handler after nearly killing two male candidates.

Ruhking has always carried the mystique of tradition, and those who choose the path are esteemed as tough and proud, despite giving up much of a normal life. Nasmin, however, made our profession seem glamorous. Darius was a better ruhker. Zahra was a finer specimen of a roc. (I may be biased, but it was true.) But none of us could move hearts like Nasmin.

More donations in the form of money and goods began to arrive from noble patrons and wealthy merchants. That year, Babak had more than enough candidates for the open apprentice positions, which made me pessimistic about how long they might last, but thanks to shipments of surplus military armor, fewer of them were injured and only two were killed. Babak used our new wealth to expand the mews and had the leaky roof over the women's quarters fixed at last.

The tour was so popular that the following year, Nasmin and the prince repeated it and visited additional satrapies they had missed the first time around. Even when not on tour, Nasmin was often called away from the mews on her own to socialize with benefactors or to educate townships. It had an effect; I began to notice that the ordinary people I encountered were more respectful than they used to be. They offered me food and drink when I passed their farmsteads and villages. They admired Zahra but knew better than to rush in to try to touch her. The children didn't hide behind their parents in fear. Sometimes they asked me eagerly, "Are you friends with Lady Nasmin and Azar, the Red Angel?"

Is that what people are calling them now? Azar had dark coloring on her primaries and tail feathers, but I wouldn't describe her as red and she was hardly an angel. More like a bad-tempered hag. I smiled and told them that yes, I was. They were delighted by this information, by my connection to celebrity.

I shouldn't have been jealous of Nasmin. No one becomes a ruhker hoping for public acclaim. Most of us barely want to talk to other people. All I'd ever wished for was to become a ruhker and hunt manticores, and now that I'd achieved that goal, I wanted to become a *better* ruhker, someone as skilled as Darius, as accomplished and respected as the most senior members of the mews. I had no desire to attend royal feasts or go on imperial tours. And the idea of winning the attention of a handsome young prince! It was foolishness.

Yet, Nasmin could be a ruhker *and* a lady. She could trek around in hunting garb and skin game, but also wear silk robes and make sparkling conversation. She had Azar, yet she didn't give up being a part of society. Her association with Prince Khovash and her role as an ambassador were raising the profile of the Royal Mews and the status of our profession. Of all of the royal ruhkers who toiled and risked our lives for the kingdom, the common people we protected knew only the names of Lady Nasmin and the Red Angel.

It would've been easier to take if I didn't miss her.

A slim letter arrived from my father, informing me that he was getting married. He was forty-six, well off, and not so old yet that he couldn't start a new family. He gave me the bare details and wrote that it would be a small, quiet ceremony. The letter was very considerate. He didn't expect me to travel all the way back to our home satrapy to attend the wedding. Now that I was a royal ruhker, I was at the king's service and didn't have much leisure time. He asked me to offer some prayers and burnt offerings instead; that would be more than enough. He prayed that I was healthy and well. If I had time, I could write him back.

I thought to do so, but my father was right, I was busy.

Tragedy can bring some people closer. At least, that's what I've heard. My father and I didn't blame each other.

We didn't exonerate each other either. It was enough that with our polite and infrequent letters, we were careful not to do any more harm.

It's difficult to convey both the variety and monotony of ruhking. There were days of hunting and days of rest. The days of rest were not in fact restful—there were always chores to do, equipment to be cleaned and repaired, new apprentices to oversee, as well as any number of things to obsess over: our rocs' weight and health and diet, the weather, reports of manticore activity, news of recent kills, injuries, deaths, sightings of wild rocs, and excitement over captured fledglings.

On hunts, more often than not, we caught nothing. It was typical for me to end such a day stewing in my own feelings of ineptitude and worthlessness. I wasn't unusual among ruhkers in my irrational certainty that there was *always* something I'd done to let down my roc. After all, Zahra was a perfect killer, so any fault must be with the incompetent monkey dragging her down.

Yet the good days sweep aside all the tedious and mediocre ones like dust off a table. Nothing compares to the feeling of riding back to the mews with a trophy tied to your chariot like a conquering hero. On those days, you feel as if you and your roc are one. Zahra and I were complete; we were the sun and the wind, the sky and the earth, life and death, above the world and untouchable.

Three years passed in this way, retained in my memory as a scattering of crystalline moments against a sprawling backdrop of days blending, one after the other. Riding out in the soft early morning light, chariot wheels churning the yellow dust and rumbling the floor under my sandals. The steadily trotting horses sending birds and insects into the air ahead of their hooves. The crisp air stinging my ears and cheeks, but gradually warming against my skin as the sun climbs over the horizon. Zahra, sitting on the cadge behind me, close enough for me to touch her breast feathers, close enough for her to punch all five talons of one foot through my back. Watching our distorted shadows sailing alongside us on the ground, her bulk looming over my small figure. Often, Darius is there alongside us with Minu, the easy sway of their figures on the moving chariot as much a part of the landscape as the vast sky and distant mountains.

When I stop the chariot and unhood Zahra, I always feel a small lurch in my chest, the moment of vertigo before jumping off a precipice into a cold lake. Every time she takes to the air, I marvel that such a huge creature can be so light and free. Rocs are a reminder that nothing is beyond God's power of creation. She is possibility incarnate; when she soars into the air, she takes part of me with her, far away from the constraints of the earth.

She was also as tedious and demanding of my patience as only a large beast can be. Unless you spend time, a great deal of time, with rocs, you cannot appreciate how individual their personalities are. When Zahra was in the mood to hunt, she was as murderously motivated a creature as can be imagined. She would go after quarry that would seem beneath her—jackals, foxes, even pheasants. I saw her chase them over open ground, pumping her enormous wings to try and cut off their unpredictable darting escapes, often times sailing right past them with unstoppable momentum. On occasion, she would even *run* after prey, with great ungainly hopping and flapping. It was almost comical to witness, like an elephant trying to dance, the foolish effort rarely successful.

At other times, however, she was like a recalcitrant child—one the size of a large man armed with deadly weapons. Thankfully, she was never hostile to me, but she could be disdainful and stubborn. When she was not in the mood to hunt, I had no way to persuade her. Once, we received a request from a landowner to cull an outsized group of wild boar that had been ruining his crops. When we found the hogs, Zahra looked straight at them for several minutes and then ignored them. She was at an optimal weight; the wind was good; the prey was easy and plentiful. I nudged the chariot closer and closer, encouraged her, uttered several choice profanities. She simply couldn't be bothered. She could also be ridiculous at times, playing with the bucket that I used to sweep up her pen, rolling it around on the ground and tapping it with her beak to make a hollow sound, or swooping down over roads to frighten travelers' carriage horses for no reason.

Sometimes, when she stared off into the distance, keen and unblinking, I imagined she was yearning for distantly remembered liberty and coming to the realization that she could easily leave me. As she entered her fourth year and came into sexual maturity, I was constantly on the watch for signs that she might not want me anymore. Rocs must learn to fly and hunt from their parents, so there were no male rocs kept in captivity for breeding. The mews was like a nunnery. When Zahra was slow returning to the sound of my whistle, I imagined her leaving to seek a more suitable companion. The idea filled me with aching fear.

I scanned the skies vigilantly for any sign of wild males before loosing her. Ruhkers have been abandoned by their rocs during this uncertain period, but usually if the partnership endures until the sixth year the roc will not leave her hunting partner, not even for one of her own kind. So I watched and guarded Zahra with all the paranoia of a jealous bridegroom. My love was entirely possessive. When you love a person, you are expected to give them their freedom, but when you love a monster, you keep it caged. A monster can't love you back, so there's none of the guilt of a reciprocal relationship. You're already subjugated. You're already holding yourself captive in a cruel way, so you justify whatever unusual bonds you level in return. I bargained with Zahra in my heart. I've already given you everything of myself. I've left my home, I've braved death, I've devoted myself to your care and training. I hunt with you and for you, I deliver all the bloodshed you crave, I worship you with my weak human frailty. In return, you must stay. You must make me worthwhile. You must be leashed to this cadge and kept in this pen, and you must never fly free as you were born to do, because I will never be free of you either, and we are partners in our captivity, each perfectly monstrous in our own way.

Very slowly, something changed between me and Darius.

The job of a ruhker is a full-time calling, one considered too dangerous to allow for marriage or children, but many of the male ruhkers kept and visited mistresses in the city, and some of them married secretly. As a strict rule, male and female ruhkers lived in separate quarters, but that did not prevent couples from forming. There were seven men for every one woman, so women apprentices and junior ruhkers were often propositioned or outright pressured, although Babak, to his credit, was intolerant of worse behavior and wouldn't hesitate to have someone whipped or expelled if they caused problems.

Nasmin and the other women had warned me early on about salacious comments, leers or innuendo, hands "accidentally" brushing against body parts, and sometimes even worse. So I wasn't unaware of what could happen, but personally, I didn't encounter any problems. Not that I wanted to, but I assumed that I simply wasn't attractive enough to merit that sort of notice from men. I had the stocky stature and large hands of a southerner. I wrapped my untamable hair in a bandana to keep it out of my face while riding in the chariot or doing chores. I don't think of myself as unfriendly but I also didn't invite much conversation. Next to Nasmin, I was as noticeable as a partridge in the grass.

Only over time did I come to suspect there was something else going on. Darius had been around me ever since I'd had Zahra. He'd met me on the path when I'd emerged from the dark days and come to watch us train the following morning. At every moment in my progression as a ruhker—Zahra's first free flight, her first hunts, her first manticore kill—Darius had been there. I'd partnered with other ruhkers as well, but I always came back to Darius.

Like me, Darius had little else in his life besides ruhking. We had lengthy and intensely detailed conversations about the ideal type of fat to use to soften jesses or the most efficient method of packing one's ruhker's bag. When we were not talking about ruhking, we barely needed to talk at all. We shared everything about our rocs—how Minu was eating, an amusing thing Zahra had done—and only a little about our families and our lives before we arrived at the mews. Once, standing over one of Zahra's kills, I confessed to Darius my personal hatred of manticores, confiding to him that my mother and little brother had been killed by one when I was thirteen years old. Another time, while sweeping out the mews, Darius mentioned he'd run away from home at age fourteen, that wild places and things had been his childhood refuge from a cruel stepfather.

We didn't bring up either topic again. Not because we avoided them, but because there was simply no need. Our pasts didn't matter when we were with each other. We had only the work, our rocs, and the hunt.

Our relationship wasn't romantic, but apparently other people didn't see it that way. I came to realize the other ruhkers assumed Darius and I were inseparable for other reasons. They thought he'd staked some unspoken claim over me. In normal society, Darius would hardly be what one would consider a prime suitor. He was gangly and unsmiling, socially reticent to the point of awkwardness, always covered with dust and smelling of animals.

Among the rarified world of the royal ruhkers, however, he was a man of status. He'd made an impression with the broken-arm incident when he was only an apprentice. He'd earned the trust of Minu, an older roc who'd already had a partner and would otherwise have to be released. He had more manticore kills to his name than anyone else near our age and within sight of some of the senior ruhkers. When Darius asked Babak for a hunting area, his flag went on the board. The other ruhkers thought I was off limits.

I didn't how to feel about that. I certainly didn't know how to feel about the faint and indistinct suspicion that perhaps their assumptions were not entirely unfounded. I'd been certain that Darius thought of me only as a friend and reliable hunting partner. He was enthralled by Zahra, not me. I was simply the unavoidable human component. Yet I began to have doubts.

One afternoon, after Minu had killed a lion and we were resting in the shade of a magnificent old cypress tree that had probably been around since before Dartha was founded, Darius told me of the first time he'd seen a roc. His family traded in animals—horses, mules, also camels and peacocks. When he was ten years old, he accompanied his uncle to the Royal Mews to deliver some horses.

"As we rode up, I saw a roc sitting on the back of a chariot with one foot on the cadge and the other resting on the body of a manticore." Darius's gaze was distant as he drew out the memory. "Her breast was pure white, and in the sun, her head and wings were as red as fire. She was like a goddess in the form of a bird, standing tall and proud. I could barely stand to look at a creature as dazzling as she was, and at the same time I couldn't look away."

He stopped and turned toward me, but though he leaned slightly forward, he didn't continue. I realized that he'd never looked at me before, not in the way he was doing now. When we were together, he was always looking away, far off across the land. His long gaze had to return from a great distance to settle on my face. Darius's regard was like the piercing stare of a roc, just as steady and unblinking, but shy and warm where a roc's is brave and cold. His deep-set eyes were so familiar to me, yet I'd never seen them up close. They were a rich, burnt brown, and when the light struck them, the specks of amber in the irises were the gold of a desert sun.

"After that moment, rocs were like a fever in my brain," Darius said at last. "I couldn't stop thinking about them. I had to be a ruhker." He hesitated. "I suppose I can be single-minded, but I just knew what I wanted."

His head tilted forward, a fractional movement. I had the sudden ridiculous impression that he was going to kiss me, and I became as still as a frightened rabbit. The thought of kissing Darius was not unpleasant, but it was such a strange idea that I didn't know how to react. I couldn't decide whether I wanted to lean forward or pull back, so I did neither. I sat still, gazing back at him dumbly.

Darius's expression didn't change, but he blinked once, slowly, as if he were coming out of a reverie and unsure of what he'd been doing before drifting off. A heartbeat passed and then the moment was gone. He pulled his long arms close to his body and rubbed his elbows, something he did when searching for words. "We'd better dress this kill and get going before the wind picks up." He gathered his bag and waterskin and stood. I got to my feet as well, relieved or disappointed, I couldn't say.

Lying alone in bed and oddly unable to sleep that night, I convinced myself that I didn't want anything to change between me and Darius. We were perfect as we were, closer to our rocs than to fellow humans. Any disruption to that equilibrium might draw us away from the shared passion that had allowed us to find our friendship in the first place. No doubt Darius felt the same way and had come to the same conclusion.

◦⟡◦

The number of captive rocs and ruhkers grew. Gazsi was only one of many roc hunters who braved their lives to bring fledglings to the mews, and each satrapy now sent two or more candidates at every call for apprentices. Babak was still the Master of the Mews but he became ever busier and more harried. He had assistants now, and a roster of deputy masters, and he spent much of his time traveling between the dozen mews that dotted every corner of the realm, positioned to cover all the wild places where manticores emerged to prey on people in growing numbers.

It was as General Zubin had said to me and Nasmin when we'd met him at the royal feast: Dartha's military victories against the barbarian tribes on the eastern border were contributing to the kingdom's expansion, establishing new trade routes and settlements in previously unoccupied territories. But the dirt roads in those outskirts of the realm were narrow and ill defended, the hastily constructed buildings flimsy, and the towns contained only low walls and minimal fortifications, if any at all. Manticores were migrating there, attracted by the prospect of easy meals.

General Zubin set some of the brightest minds in the army to the task of coming up with improved ways to trap and kill the man-eaters. Strong nets dropped from trees, pits lined with spikes, armored pikemen with wicked sickles shaped like roc's talons on the end of their long weapons.

Some ruhkers murmured that the army was trying to put us out of a job. I didn't see it that way. As manticore hunters, we ought to welcome anything that aided us in our purpose. Besides, all of Zubin's new methods required intensive manpower, training, equipment. They were at best a defensive measure. There was still nothing else that could hunt down a manticore like a roc. Nothing else could strike like a bolt from the sky, like the punishing hand of God.

The growing awareness of this might've made people appreciate ruhkers more, but it also made them complacent and entitled. I had experienced the frustrated glare of landowners when Zahra frightened their herds or failed to kill the wolves they complained about. But that was nothing compared to the accusatory anger of communities who lost residents and people who lost loved ones because of attacks they now thought preventable.

"I'm thankful I've been able to bring rocs and ruhking into the hearts of the common people," Nasmin said to me in a moment of exasperation, "but they don't understand that we can't be everywhere at once. They still have to take responsibility for their own safety. Instead, when an attack occurs, they shout, 'Where was the Red Angel when we needed her?' That's what they demand to know, as if it's my fault there aren't a thousand Azars flying over every bit of Dartha!"

◦⌒◦

In the fortieth year of his reign, Antrius the Bold announced a Great Hunt. The eastern satrapies were to be made safe from the predation of the Deceiver's spawn.

The famed Third Division under the command of General Zubin would conduct a joint campaign with the Royal Mews to kill as many manticores as could be found, making the countryside safe for the citizens of the kingdom.

In the map room, Babak, a little heavier in the middle these days but his graying beard neatly braided, stood next to the more physically imposing General Zubin as they explained our mission. Twenty of the best teams from the Royal Mews would accompany the Third Division as it traveled eastward. The army would search the countryside by marching in long lines. Rocs would watch from the sky, ready to stoop to kill any manticores that appeared. Well-armored soldiers with long pikes would fight manticores up close if need be, but God willing, the king's sharp-eyed, hungry rocs would prevent it from happening too often.

"One day, we'll hunt down every last manticore in the realm and the people of Dartha will finally live free from fear of those horrible spawn," General Zubin declared. "The Great Hunt will be a monumental step toward that day."

We all applauded General Zubin's dream, but despite my long personal hatred of manticores, I didn't feel his words in my heart. I don't believe manticores can ever be wiped out, but if they somehow were, then there would be no further need for the Royal Mews. If I lived to see such an unlikely day, I'd be witnessing the end of my own usefulness.

"I don't like it," Darius said out loud, after General

Zubin had departed the mews. Everyone in the briefing room looked at him. Darius didn't speak up very often in a crowd. "Our rocs will be too close to each other. And there'll be too many people and distractions."

Several of the other ruhkers nodded in agreement. Rocs hunt alone and do not take well to sharing airspace. The army's involvement would mean lots of people and horses, noise and overstimulation. A soldier getting too close to an irritated raptor; a hungry roc deciding to go after one of the horses; a discomfited bird simply not being willing to hunt at a crucial moment—any of those things could lead to tragic consequences.

Babak acknowledged our concerns but explained they would not stop the Great Hunt from proceeding. Thanks to Prince Khovash's enthusiasm for ruhking and the fame of Nasmin and the Red Angel, the whole kingdom knew that rocs were the best weapon against manticores. Our orders came from the king, who wasn't willing to send out thousands of soldiers on a hunt without rocs in the air to help them. Babak advocated with Zubin for the rocs to be flown in shorter shifts, with positional signals sent up between the units of the Third Division to ensure proper distancing. Roomy crates would be brought along on wagons so our birds could rest and sleep in sheltered surroundings protected from the onslaught of unfamiliar sights and sounds. A small detail of attendants would provide assistance to the ruhkers and see to it that the rocs were not disturbed by soldiers or curious civilians. It was about all we could ask for.

Despite our misgivings, we couldn't help being excited as well. The Great Hunt was a bold event, the largest coordinated drive to eradicate manticores that anyone could remember. The announcement of it energized the citizens, especially in the eastern satrapies, filling them with the reassurance that we are not helpless creatures huddling in fear, waiting for predators to strike. It was the monsters who ought to fear us. For too long, General Zubin argued, we'd been reacting instead of attacking. He promised that manticore skulls would hang over every gate of the realm's border outposts to hearten travelers and frighten invaders. The Great Hunt would show everyone that manticores might look like demons, but they were still animals that could be brought down by our God-given power to harness nature.

It was a courageous and inspiring thing to say. It was also arrogant in a way not unique to Dartha, or to kings or generals of any place. Any defiance of the wild leads at best to a fragile, temporary victory. Nature and fate are their own capricious monsters, ones that cannot be tamed any more than a roc ever truly belongs to her ruhker.

IV

SAVIOR

The Great Hunt got underway at the dry end of the summer of my sixth year as a ruhker. A procession of chariots carrying twenty rocs and their handlers journeyed east for four days to join General Zubin's Third Division. A thousand men in ten companies would march through the eastern satrapies like the teeth of a comb running through a head of hair for lice, searching out and killing manticores.

The night before we departed the mews, I spoke to Zahra in her pen as I fed her camel meat and refreshed her water. "Let's add at least one kill to our names, my lady."

Every ruhker believes their bird is superior, but there are only so many chances for our rocs to shine and for us to bask in their glory. Innumerable tedious hours are spent training and hunting, leading to a few crucial seconds to prove oneself, and those seconds are often determined by sheer luck. Ruhkers are a small, tight-knit community of willingly outcast obsessives. We all work toward the same goal and support each other, but we're competitive as well.

Zahra bobbed on the perch as if in agreement. As long

as the conditions were good and we got our chance, she would surely not fail.

Darius and I were attached to Yellow Company. Their commander was a tall man named Omid who had pale eyes and a nose hooked like a hawk's beak. In front of his men, Omid was gruff and confident, but he admitted privately to us that he'd never encountered a manticore before, and most of his men hadn't either. He wished to keep it that way. "We joined the army to fight men, not beasts," he grumbled. "These boys are willing to die for Dartha, but being eaten is another matter." He explained that they'd been given two weeks' worth of training on how to encircle and bring down a manticore, but he was worried that confronting one of the monsters in the flesh might undo even the most disciplined soldier.

I could understand his concern. Even if the men didn't scream or run, how effective could they be against a manticore? I imagined a lion surrounded by rabbits holding sharpened sticks. The success of the Great Hunt depended on soldiers flushing out the monsters and holding them at bay so rocs could finish them off from the sky. The entire Third Division was playing the part of a ruhker. "Let's pray that Zahra's and Minu's sharp eyes and appetite find any manticores well before they find us," I told Omid.

We saw nothing for the first four days of the hunt. The soldiers marched. They sang songs and shouted war chants to attract the monsters, but mostly to allay boredom. I was no stranger to long days of travel, but I wasn't used to the noise and *smell* of an army. Clouds of dust and biting flies rose up around feet and horses' hooves. The sun beat down relentlessly on the dry landscape and the sweaty men stopped to rest in the middle of the day, loosening their stinking armor and washing down dry rations with mouthfuls of water in whatever shade they were able to find.

Darius and I drove in our chariots at the center of their column. We sent Minu and Zahra into the sky in turns. We saw no sign of manticores. Minu stooped for a fallow deer; it bounded into cover and Darius whistled long and angrily, calling his disappointed roc back to the cadge. Zahra was equally annoyed that we were not providing her with worthy game. On the fourth day, she began to drift farther away on the wind. If she wandered over a neighboring company, she might encounter another roc. Nasmin and Prince Khovash were also part of this grand expedition, naturally, and I didn't want Zahra tangling with bad-tempered Azar. I thundered my chariot after Zahra, blowing the reed whistle insistently, terrified she wasn't going to respond. She did, taking her time turning a large, petulant circle in the sky before coming back toward me. On the way, she made a sudden dive and took an eagle out of the sky, almost spitefully it seemed. She carried it back to the chariot and mantled over the cadge, tearing apart one of her own kind. She'd caught a golden eagle, a regal creature, now a heartbreaking bundle of brown and white feathers. Its dead eye stared up in betrayal.

Messengers on horseback galloped between the units of the Third Division, carrying news and issuing instructions from General Zubin. We learned that Bronze

Company had found and killed two manticores already. Black Company had encountered one, but it had escaped and was now being pursued.

I vibrated with frustration. I wanted those manticores for myself and Zahra. My instinct was to rush to where the game was, not hold my place in line with Yellow Company, which the manticores seemed to be ignoring.

Captain Omid did not share my sentiment. He was glad none of his men had been carried away by razored jaws. "God willing, this will turn out to be nothing more than a long hike in the country and we won't have to get anywhere near those spawn of the Deceiver," he mumbled over the campfire.

Omid's premature optimism finally attracted the evil attention we were waiting for. The next morning, we awoke to discover that two men had disappeared during the night, snatched right off their bedrolls.

The men had been sleeping beyond the edge of camp, overconfident after four days without any sign of danger. Perhaps they'd been lovers who'd snuck out of sight of the posted sentries in search of some privacy, only to meet with a tragic and gruesome end. Darius examined the disturbed area and explained to Captain Omid that, given the size of the tracks and drag marks, it could only have been the work of a manticore.

Yellow Company had been fortunate. The sleeping men

had died instantly, without any time to make a sound. If they'd awoken screaming, the camp would've been alerted, but the manticore would've gone into a killing frenzy and there would've been many more casualties. Perhaps the monster could've been surrounded and slain in the dark, but the toll would've been great. Darius and I wouldn't have been able to help at all, as our rocs could only hunt during the day. Although the manticore had gotten away with two men, now that the sun was up, the tables were turned. We had our rocs and thus the advantage.

The attitudes of the soldiers changed at once. Fear crackled through their ranks, but with it came the alertness and discipline that had begun to wane over the past couple of days. They rushed to don armor and weapons. Some began to pray. Captain Omid swung onto his roan stallion, barking orders.

Darius and I ran for our chariots. The countryside was fairly flat, but we harnessed our horses and drove up a low rise we'd passed shortly before making camp yesterday evening. Even a small amount of elevation would be helpful. Sensing my eagerness and the urgency with which we sped across the ground, Zahra sat up on the cadge, puffing her chest out. She shook her tail feathers. When we pulled to a stop, her erect bearing presaged bloodshed.

Minu, equally capable but older, sleepier, and perhaps less easily roused to excitement, was still a little hunched on her chariot cadge, as if unimpressed by being so rudely awakened. Many an egotistical ruhker would expect to fly

their roc first if they could claim seniority over their partner. Darius was one of the best ruhkers in the kingdom
because he saw only the hunt before him: the conditions
of the birds, the wind and weather, the lay of the land, the
quarry. I didn't even need to open my mouth to argue for
Zahra; he took one look at her and said, "Fly her."

As soon as I untethered her and pulled off the hood,
Zahra took to the air like a rock from a slingshot, rocking
the chariot back on its axles as she launched herself away
from the cadge. It took her a few seconds to get completely
airborne; the wind created by the furious beating of her
immense wings slapped grass and dirt against the side of
the carriages before she snapped them out and soared away
from us, her enormous shadow speeding across the plain.

We turned the horses around and galloped back to Yellow Company. By now, the soldiers had broken camp and
scrambled into formation with impressive speed. Omid's
trackers agreed with Darius that the manticore was unlikely to have traveled more than three or four parasangs
after taking its meal. With plentiful prey nearby, it was
likely to hang about not far from the campsite with
plans to return. Scouts were sent ahead to follow the
trail left by the bodies of their unfortunate comrades.

An hour of marching brought us upon the remains of
the disappeared soldiers. There wasn't much left to find;
they had been without armor or boots, sleeping lightly
clothed in the warm night. One of them had been nearly
completely devoured. The second soldier's head, hands,
and feet were left behind. Some of the manticore's appetite

had been sated by that point and it had left the small, bony parts uneaten, like a rich child carelessly discarding the browned edges of a piece of flatbread.

I heard this from Darius. I had no desire to view the grisly remains myself. I stayed in the chariot, monitoring Zahra's position and focusing on the hunt. A soldier, a young man no older than sixteen, stumbled past me and vomited into a clump of bushes.

We proceeded carefully now, the soldiers tightly gripping their spears. At any moment, without warning, the long leonine bulk of the monster might glide out of the tall grass, or spring out from behind the cover of low trees and shrubs into our midst like a cat into a birdbath. I kept the horses moving forward at the same pace as the men, my eyes on the sky. Zahra was turning great circles above us. She could easily stay up there all day, barely moving her enormous wings, the warm updraft keeping her aloft. It was far easier for her to remain in the sky than to land and take off again. She would follow my chariot wherever it went, relying on the promise that I would flush out a meal for her.

But her patience was limited. I'd trained her with lures and meat to want manticore more than any other prey, but if too much time passed, she would get bored and annoyed at my failure to deliver. I had to estimate when that might happen and call her back to the chariot with the promise of meat from my bag, or she would go after something easier—a deer, a leopard, a jackal—if she spotted it first. Or else she might fly away to land on some distant outcropping, potentially costing me hours to go after her, begging her to return. Either way, we would lose valuable time and then she might not want to hunt again. We couldn't afford for that to happen today, not with lives at stake.

Darius leaned across from his chariot and tapped the side of mine to get my attention. "She's got the fire in her today. She looks steady." He knew exactly what I'd been thinking, had easily read my anxiety because it was what he'd be feeling if Minu were in the sky. I brought my eyes down to meet his, relaxing a little and nodding gratefully at his reassurance. It was true; Zahra was focused and eager. I knew my roc. I had already done everything I could, through every moment of doggedly patient training over the years. She would bring down the manticore if only we could find it. That part was up to all of us, including the soldiers.

Captain Omid said, "If we keep following the beast south, we might run into Blue Company." He sent a messenger on horseback galloping off to warn the neighboring unit that a manticore was headed their way and to inform the other captain of our position and direction of travel. The two companies might be able to close in on the monster's location from opposite sides, so long as it didn't slip between us. I told Omid's messenger that if Blue Company was near us that they should not send up a roc, and if one was already in the air, then to call her down so her presence would not distract Zahra.

We encountered difficult terrain—a sloping ravine that dropped down into a dry creek bed at the bottom and then rose steeply on the other side before flattening

into open scrubland. Darius and I regarded the imped-
iment with dismay. The manticore's direction of travel
led straight through the gully, but the wheels of the light
ruhker's chariots couldn't navigate the rocky ground. We
would have to detour at least a parasang out of the way.
It would take far too much time for Yellow Company to
circle the area on foot along with us; we would lose the
trail unless they crossed the gully here. However, Zahra
would follow my chariot, which meant the soldiers would
be without protection from the air as they picked their
way over to the other side.

"We'll travel in stages," Darius explained to Captain
Omid. He would take Minu in his chariot and travel
around the gulch as quickly as he could. I would wait
here with Zahra overhead as the soldiers made their way
across. After Omid and his men joined up with Darius on
flat ground on the other side, I would call Zahra down,
and Darius would send up Minu. Then I would follow Darius's chariot tracks to catch up with them. The plan would
slow our progress, but it was the safest way to proceed.

Darius whipped his horses, throwing up a trail of dust
that fogged the shape of Minu's perched, hulking form as
it receded into the distance. I remained in my chariot and
kept shifting my attention between my roc in the sky and
the soldiers beginning their march down into the ravine.
It was for the best that I call Zahra down soon. She was
still directly overhead but drifting lower, her circles noticeably tightening. She was being patient with me, but
she had been in the air for more than two hours and I

could sense that she wanted to land and feed. "Just a little longer, my lady," I whispered.

The soldiers crossed the creek bed, dry as a bone after a long summer, and began climbing up the other side. Some of them were leading horses, which slowed them further. They were doing their best to stay together, but at times they had to scramble on all fours, lugging gear and weapons, and their normally perfect lines became jagged.

They were halfway up the slope when the monster appeared.

One of the reasons some say the manticore is the physical manifestation of the Deceiver is because at times it seems to possess an evil intelligence equal to our own. It considers how its prey behaves. It chooses when and how to strike to inspire the most fear and chaos. The manticore had lain motionless, its gray-brown pelt hiding it completely among the rocks and shrubbery while the company marched past. Only when the men thought they'd made it past potential danger, when they were strung out in a broken line on unstable ground, unable to stand shoulder to shoulder and fight to defend themselves, did it emerge. From higher ground, I saw the beast before the soldiers did. My stomach plummeted as I watched it sweep toward the men with silent, terrifying surety, its massive paws soundless on the rocks, its tooth-filled ape face grinning wide with the promise of death.

The worst thing you can do when you see a manticore is to make noise, but I had no choice. "Manticore!"

I screamed in warning. "Run! *Run!* Get to the top and don't scream!"

The manticore paused, attracted by the sound of my voice. Its shaggy black head turned, its demonic gaze traveling upward, fixing on me. An icy wave of recognition seemed to suck away the heat of the blazing sun and weld me to the floor of the chariot. The manticore's black tongue lolled between its long teeth. Like a dog, it tilted its head at me with curiosity. I stared into mismatched eyes—one of them brown, the other bright blue.

This could not be the monster from my childhood. That manticore had been in a completely different part of the country and was long dead by now. Mismatched eye color is not so rare in animals. My mind knew this, but my heart did not. In one horrible moment, I was standing outside my childhood home again, my fist stuffed into my mouth, piss running down my legs, staring at the one sandal on the road and the other dangling in the air.

Then Yellow Company did what I'd told them not to do. They saw the manticore and some of them screamed. Their voices drowned out mine. The monster swung its attention back to the soldiers, now clambering for their lives up the slope, sending small stones tumbling down behind them. They needed to get out of the gully onto flat ground where they could stand together and fight. Exposed like this, they would be easily picked off. The beast bounded toward the men, covering the distance with terrifying speed, its thick barbed tail stabilizing its sure-footed ascent. It would be on them in seconds.

Zahra swooped down over the lip of the ravine so close to me that the tips of her primaries nearly grazed the chariot. She exceeded the manticore's soundless menace, streaking toward her target with a deadly grace that I'd witnessed countless times but which never failed to suck the breath from my body in awe. Salvation from above.

The manticore sensed its doom arrowing from the sky. It broke off its pursuit of the soldiers and turned, quilled pelt flared all over its body, black lips pulled back over its hideous mouth. Zahra's platter-sized feet with their sickle toes reached for the manticore's neck.

At the last possible instant, the beast leapt straight up into the air to avoid Zahra's killing strike. Her talons missed the manticore by less than a finger's length. The whole thing seemed to unfold in slow motion. I felt as though my very soul leapt from my body to my roc. I was Zahra. I was the one who missed my mark. I was the one who barreled into the slope at full speed, bruising myself tumbling into the hillside in a barrage of feathers.

Zahra righted herself. Hissing and flapping, she hopped after the manticore, still determined to reach it, but on the ground, there was no contest as to which monster was faster. The manticore was no longer interested in the soldiers and wanted only to get away from Zahra's bone-cracking wings and dismembering talons. It reached the top of the gully in two enormous bounds and fled.

Zahra sat with her wings and beak open, looking di-sheveled, murderously disappointed, and tired. Hot tears of frustration were streaming down my face. I blew the reed whistle. I had to blow it twice before she returned to the chariot, in a series of flapping hops rather than flight. I fed her hunks of camel meat from my bag, a poor consolation for a lost kill, but she snatched the pieces out of my gloved hand and ate ravenously. I told her she'd done her best. She'd done everything she could. She'd saved those soldiers' lives and mine. It had been a difference of seconds and inches, a case of the fateful luck that reigns supreme between every hunter and hunted thing.

The soldiers of Yellow Company were recovering their bearings after staring death in the face. They were climbing out of the ravine, and the braver among them were running ahead on Omid's shouted orders to keep the manticore in sight and track its direction of travel. I was still sunken in our failure when I saw the unmistakable silhouette of a roc sweeping toward our position with the late-morning sun at its tail. I shielded my eyes and broke into a grin. It was Minu. I could recognize her pure white breast even at this distance.

Darius! Sharp-eyed Darius, his eyes always on the sky. He would've seen Zahra stoop, then immediately heard me blowing the reed whistle, calling her back to the chariot. He would've understood at once that the manticore had evaded my roc, and without wasting a moment, he'd sent Minu into the sky. Now, squinting into the distance, I could make out the plume of dust from his chariot wheels. The manticore couldn't be far. The hunt was still on.

I leashed Zahra to the cadge, hooded her, and whipped the horses to a gallop, racing after Darius to circle the gully. Darius's chariot tracks were easy to follow in the dry dirt and trampled yellow grass, but it was beyond frustrating that every turn of the wheels was taking me away from the action. If only I had wings to carry me there as swiftly as a roc. I tried to keep Minu's silhouette in my sight even as she disappeared occasionally behind the copses of trees that I passed in a rush. She was circling, focused, her keen eyes searching. Any trace of the lethargy she'd shown first thing that morning had vanished. Minu was an old warrior. Across her partnership with two ruhkers over twenty-one years, she'd killed more manticores than any other roc in the Royal Mews. She was a seasoned hunter, and Darius was a masterful trainer. If anyone could find and kill the manticore where Zahra and I had failed, it would be them. I wanted to be there to see it.

At last, the ravine ended and I swung the horses around and sent them running toward where Yellow Company had crossed. When I finally pulled alongside Captain Omid's stallion, he pointed into a stand of oak. "It's in there." Darius's chariot was driving along the outskirts of the trees, with Minu waiting overhead until she had a clear path of attack.

Omid's men approached the woods in a tight formation, manticore-killing pikes extended, showing much more discipline and bravery than I'd expected after seeing their panic back in the ravine. That experience seemed to have shamed and motivated them. Now they had a prideful desire to take down the manticore for themselves, not wanting to be known for accomplishing nothing on the Great Hunt besides losing their composure and being saved by a giant bird. They were making a great deal of noise, rattling their weapons and shouting profanities, taunting the manticore, daring it to come out.

The monster wasn't taking the bait. Perhaps it had been shaken by the encounter with Zahra. We would have to get close enough to draw it out of the trees. Omid set his jaw determinedly and kicked his horse forward, ordering his men to continue their advance. I stared hard into the shadows between the tree trunks, not sure if the movement I glimpsed was the manticore's mottled pelt, or the motion of branches in the wind, or merely my imagination. My mouth was dry as sand and sweat trickled down my neck and under my collar.

A messenger on horseback appeared suddenly from around the other side of the oak stand, galloping toward us at top speed, waving a scarf over his head to get our attention. "You're too close!" he shouted when he neared. "Blue Company's roc is in the air. Halt your advance and bring your bird down."

Captain Omid swung around angrily to meet the man. "I sent a messenger to inform them that *we* were tracking the manticore south. We have the brute trapped in these trees, and we intend to bring it out and put an end to it. Have Blue Company call down *their* roc and wait for—"

The manticore shot out of the woods at a dead run. The brave soldiers bellowed in defiant challenge and stood their ground against the charging demon, but like a cat jumping a fence, it leapt clear over the wall of bristling pikes and landed behind the formation, knocking half a dozen men aside with a vicious lash of its barbed tail. If not for their armor, they would've died quickly from stab wounds or slowly from poison. Their comrades rushed to pull them to safety and regroup, but the manticore was no longer in any mood to fight or to eat, only to escape. It ignored everyone and ran in the direction the rider had come from.

Minu was waiting. As soon as the manticore was in the open, she folded her wings and dove. There was none of the rocky slope or awkward angles that Zahra had contended with earlier; Minu had all the advantage of terrain. In the roc's deathly shadow, the manticore put on a burst of speed. Minu hit the monster in the forequarters with the force of a boulder hurled from heaven. Both monsters went to the ground in a tangle of quills and feathers, fearsome snarling and flapping and terrific violence. Minu's scaly talons were buried in the manticore's shoulder and she was battering it with her wings as it heaved and writhed on the ground, trying to reach her with its jaws, slashing wildly with its tail as she sunk her grip deep into its flesh. My heart was beating so loudly in my throat that I couldn't open it to make a sound. Darius's chariot was racing toward the fight.

When I was thirteen years old, I learned that when disaster arrives, it does so without omen or portent. The truly terrible moments strike us the way a roc strikes its prey—without warning, out of the clear blue sky.

Another roc came sailing over the trees like an arrow and fell upon Minu with a shriek of territorial fury. It

seems impossible that a man-sized bird can come out of
nowhere, but that's how it seemed to happen. In a moment
of vertigo-inducing disbelief and horror, I recognized the
attacker. *Azar.* Nasmin's roc. Her talons were raking Minu's
face and she was screaming with rage, her wings buffeting
the older bird. I'd only ever seen rocs in the mews issuing warning displays to each other, hissing, erect, wings
stretched. Those few instances had been terrifying to witness, but they'd never turned into full-on battles. They
hadn't been like this. This was unbridled wrath.

Poor Minu fell back, confused, her eye streaming blood.
She lost her grip on the struggling manticore. It whipped
its head around and crunched its jaws over the top of
her wing.

Darius let out a howl as he heard his roc's wing bone
crack. I'd never heard such a noise from him before. It
sounded more animal than human. He was out of his
chariot before he could even pull the horses to a complete
halt. Stumbling as he landed, he drew his akinaka and
sprinted into the three-way battle of monsters, heedless
of his own safety.

I was out of my own chariot and running helplessly after
him, screaming. *"Darius! Darius!"* Omid's soldiers were following him and shouting as well, but he didn't once glance
behind or wait for help from any of us. We were too far
away to do anything except watch. That moment is scored
indelibly into my mind—Darius plunging into the chaos
like a rabbit between snarling wolves, his long, tanned
limbs unprotected, thinking only to save his partner.

He got between Minu and Azar. Somehow, he seized Azar's loose jesses and pulled her to the ground away from his roc. In the storm of movement, one of the manticore's flailing clawed feet struck Darius square in the chest. I saw an arc of blood spray the grass as my friend was thrown backward. He landed on his side and lay unmoving, still clutching Azar's jesses for the sake of his roc's life.

I stumbled and fell to my knees in the dirt, my mind an unending white shriek of denial. The manticore twisted its long body, regained its feet, and ran, limping, away from all of us. In seconds, it was lost to sight and I was once again left only with the carnage of its passing.

Darius was broken.

Three of his ribs were fractured. The deep parallel gashes across his chest cost him an almost fatal amount of blood. He'd struck his head on the ground and been knocked senseless by the manticore's blow. An army field medic stitched his wounds and bound his torso in bandages. He was laid in the back of a supply wagon and rushed to the nearest town, where he was placed in an inn and attended to by a proper doctor.

I hovered like a spirit around my friend's bedside or outside the door to the room. When Darius burned with fever, I wrung out cold washcloths and placed them on his face and chest. I left only to attend to Zahra, who was crated in the inn's stable. I stroked her wings and wept, my tears falling and rolling off her smooth feathers. She couldn't comfort me with words or affection, but her presence was what I needed most. I didn't need to hold back my feelings around her; monsters aren't weakened by human grief.

Prince Khovash arrived in his gilded carriage with his attendants and his own personal physician who examined Darius and gave instructions for his care. The prince spoke to me with solemn, heartfelt concern. Darius and I were both heroes of Dartha. Khovash would ask his father to issue us royal commendations. He promised he would personally visit the Fire Temple to burn sandalwood and instruct the magi to pray for the brave ruhker's recovery. I thanked the lord prince with my head bowed and felt not the slightest urge to raise my eyes to look upon his face. The magnetic draw of his bright and earnest beauty, the thrill of even his slight attention and the validation that his approving smile had always seemed to promise—they were insubstantial and always had been.

When Darius awoke, he said weakly, "Minu."

I had to tell him. If it were my roc, I would need to know. Minu's life as a hunter was over, but Babak, who deep down loved rocs as much as any of us, had tried to save her anyway. Four ruhkers in heavy armor had held Minu down, patched her eye, splinted her wing. But the manticore's poison was in her blood, slowing her old heart. She'd died two days later, only a few hours before Darius awoke.

I told Darius this with gentle words and terror wrapped around my heart. I knew what would happen next. Emptiness came into my friend's eyes, turning them as blank as white limestone. I could see the will to live draining out of him like spring runoff. I pressed his hand and called his name. Darius closed his eyes and didn't answer. He sank back into unconsciousness and tried to stay under. I dragged him back to the surface, rousing him every few hours to change his bandages, dribbling broth and soft food into his mouth. He fought me like a tethered bird bating from the perch, weakly turning his head away, resisting my care with limpness. "Leave me alone," he moaned. "Just let me die."

I refused. I bent every ounce of the determination and patience that a ruhker has for taming a monster into coaxing Darius away from following his roc. It was selfish of me. If it had been me in Darius's place, if it had been Zahra dead and wrapped in white instead of Minu, I would've hated anyone who tried to convince me that I had any further obligation to this world. I was Zahra's ruhker. That's all I was. Darius and I were alike. What can you offer to someone who's lost their purpose, their own sense of worth?

But I was nothing if not selfish. Ruhkers are captors, after all.

Nasmin, when she came to the inn, was barely recognizable. The warm bronze color in her cheeks was missing, the curls in her dark tresses were limp, the sunny confidence I'd so admired was nowhere to be seen. "She wouldn't come to me." Nasmin wept. "I thought she would always come."

When Blue Company received the message Captain Omid had sent to them, Azar had been in the air for only ten minutes. She wouldn't return to the chariot when Nasmin called her down. She'd drifted north, forcing her ruhker to race after her, blowing the whistle desperately to lure her back.

Stubborn, bad-tempered Azar was a superlative hunter, but she hadn't been flown regularly enough. Azar had made many public appearances but hadn't had a manticore kill to her name for over a year. The expectations and celebrity of being a public spokeswoman and the prince's romantic interest had consumed most of Nasmin's time and attention. When she was away from the mews, other ruhkers had done the daily labor of exercising and feeding Azar. In the moment when it mattered most and the consequences were truly dire, her roc did not listen to her. The meat on the cadge was not enough, and the habit of obeying Nasmin's commands had dimmed. From many parasangs away, Azar saw Minu hunting manticore and her blood rose, the instinctive territorial fury of a queen. The sky was her territory and she would stomach no rivals.

I sat across from Nasmin and didn't know what to say. I wanted to scream that this was all her fault. I wanted to wrap my arms around her and assure her that she needn't blame herself. Neither would've been true, nor fair. In the end, I wanted only to weep with her, and I was already too wrung out to even do that. Perhaps my father had looked at me across an empty table all those years ago and felt the way that I did now.

"I'm sorry," I said, because I was.

I thought Darius was asleep, but when Nasmin left, he turned on his side, back to the door.

I've never hated Nasmin for what happened. All through our friendship, I'd looked up to her and envied her, wishing I could possess her seemingly effortless ability not only as a ruhker but as a woman who could turn heads with her beauty and hearts with her charm. I thought she could do everything. Our one trip to Antopolis together had been a dream that I was only permitted to stay in for one night but that she continued living without me.

We cannot know the price others pay for their good fortune.

The entire tragic accident was kept quiet. It wouldn't do to have the name of Lady Nasmin and the Red Angel sullied among the aristocrats and commoners who admired them as symbols of our kingdom's proud tradition of ruhking. Prince Khovash didn't want to mar the Great Hunt or his own reputation, and Babak certainly didn't want to jeopardize the money that the mews received from either rich patrons or the royal court. But every ruhker in the mews knew what happened. They might not openly condemn Nasmin for losing control of her roc, but they would never trust her again.

Nasmin took Azar and moved to one of the northern

outposts. Not long thereafter, she retired the Red Angel with much public fanfare, taking Azar into the remote mountains and releasing her into the wild. The last I heard, Nasmin was married to a wealthy spice merchant and had three children. Their goods are fairly well known, so it seems my old friend is happy and doing well for herself. But as I now know, there's simply no way to tell.

Perhaps I should've been kinder to Nasmin that day, as she'd once been kind to me when I needed kindness. I imagine she'll carry invisible scars as deep as Darius's for the rest of her life. There is no worse feeling as a ruhker than knowing that your roc doesn't respect you, that it would rather hunt alone than obey you. None of Nasmin's other superlative qualities mattered to Azar. It is harder to please a roc than a prince.

Darius recovered, slowly and against his will. Prince Khovash had seen to it that our lodgings were paid for from the royal purse, so we were allowed to stay in the town's inn as long as we needed. After all, Darius was a wounded hero of the Great Hunt. I was careful not to inform him of this irony.

The Great Hunt continued without us. Over the course of two weeks, sixteen manticores in the eastern satrapies were found and killed. Eight soldiers lost their lives and twenty-one were injured. One roc was slain and her ruhker badly wounded. Darius and Minu were rolled into the total casualty number, which was reported by the court of Antrius the Bold as a tragic but worthy sacrifice, a tiny fraction of the lives taken or ruined by the evil beasts and small compared to the number saved.

Publicly, the Great Hunt was deemed a success. Villagers in the area breathed sighs of relief and cheered the returning Third Division. Celebratory feasts were held. Children waved toy rocs made of paper and string. The skulls of slain manticores were mounted over imperial gates to intimidate the king's enemies. Across the region, it seemed people were happy with the king's measures to ensure their safety. They believed the problem of manticores had been solved by human skill and ingenuity.

People have short memories, but nature is patient and implacable. The Great Hunt had made the eastern satrapies safer for a few years. More people would move there to settle the borderlands of the realm. The villages would grow into towns and more merchants would travel the roads. The townsfolk would forget their fears; they would neglect their walls and leave their children to play in the woods by themselves. And the manticores would return.

That was not for me to worry about now. The only manticore on my mind was the one that had escaped Yellow Company. I asked every ruhker who came to see Darius if the beast had been caught. "One of its front legs was injured," I said. "It had one brown eye and one blue." No one recalled seeing a manticore like that, but they supposed it might well have been taken down by someone else; they couldn't be sure. Or perhaps it had fled the area or died of its injuries.

I carried on these muted conversations in the hallway of the inn or in the courtyard beside the stables. Darius didn't want to talk to visitors. He barely talked to me. The people who came hoping to offer him comfort could only do the opposite. They still had their rocs. He didn't.

I took Zahra out alone, into the surrounding countryside, and flew her on easy game—wolves, leopards, the occasional deer. I'd never before felt lonely when I was with Zahra, but for the first time, her company was not enough. I missed Darius with the sharp grief of knowing he could not join me. When I returned from hunting, I would find him sitting on a stone bench behind the inn, a blanket wrapped around his bony shoulders, staring into nothing. He had always been thin, but strong as green wood. Now he seemed as brittle as a branch in winter.

"Why are you still here?" he asked dully.

Nearly two months had passed. The air was cooling as autumn sped by, flocks of storks winging southward, the leaves of the elm trees changing color then falling. Wild rocs would be following the migrating herds of deer and camels. Hungry manticores would be prowling close to roads and towns, eager to fatten themselves up on unlucky victims. I couldn't keep Zahra in the inn's stables indefinitely. The innkeeper was clearly impatient for me to take my creature and leave, as Zahra frightened the travelers' horses. I needed to return to the mews and my duties.

"We'll go when you're ready," I told Darius.

He shook his head angrily, his hair falling into his eyes. "I can't hunt with you. I can barely walk without getting winded. I'm not a ruhker anymore, and you have Zahra to think of." He turned away from me. His grief lay on him as thick and undisturbed as fresh snow. "Go back to the mews. I'm not someone you ought to be around."

I wanted to tell him he was wrong. This season of desolation would end. His broken bones would mend. He would regain his strength. In the spring, Gazsi and other roc hunters would arrive at the mews with new fledglings. There would be another roc for him to train, another wild thing to love. You'll hunt again, Darius. As long as your heart beats, you'll be a ruhker. I know this as much as God knows every creature, because I once thought there was no reason for me to be alive, no logic to survival, no meaning to be found past endurance of loss, yet there was. Zahra was not yet in my life, but she would be. She answered the question in my soul and made me worthwhile. And you were not yet in my life either, but then you came into it. You're part of the answer and even without your roc, you're worth more to me than you could ever know. I should've let you kiss me that one time in the field, but I was scared, and if you ever feel the urge to do it again, I would want you to.

I didn't say any of that. It wasn't what he needed to hear.

Darius was right about one thing. I couldn't pass the season here; I had to return to the mews where Zahra could winter comfortably. I tried again to suggest he come with me, but I didn't push. Returning to the mews, seeing all the ruhkers and their birds going about their usual routines, might be too much for him, might tear open the wounds that needed to heal. I couldn't decide the proper time for him. I could only do what was right for Zahra.

On a late autumn morning when I could no longer put it off, I called Zahra to the chariot and began the four-day trip back to the Royal Mews. My last sight of Darius was him standing in the doorway of the inn, his long arms at his sides, watching me go. His roughened hands were empty. Darius's hands were not meant to be empty; they were always at work, they were always full of jesses or reins, skinning knives and lures, gloves and meat. If only people were as simple and instinctive as raptors. I wished for a special reed whistle around my neck that I could blow to call him back.

Follow me.

He did not follow.

I wasn't afraid of traveling alone. I had enough provisions for the journey, the weather was still good, and as a royal ruhker, I was a considered by the law of the land to be a direct servant of the king. Any highwayman who wasn't dissuaded by the sight of the giant raptor I traveled with and tried to rob or harm me would be subject to the same penalty of execution as if they attacked a court official or stole the king's gold. Wild beasts would not approach. So it was a quiet trip, full of swaying hours interspersed only with breaks for the horses and for Zahra to stretch her wings. Plenty of time to sit with my thoughts and my sadness, with the lonely silence that was Darius's absence.

On the first two nights I found a clearing and slept rolled in a blanket next to the chariot. On the third night I was longing for a hot meal and a bath, so as dusk neared, I drove into a town and asked the first friendly-looking person I happened upon to point me to the inn.

The woman gasped, nearly dropping her basket of vegetables. Her face lit with relief. "You must be here to help us with the manticore!" she exclaimed. "But how did you get here so quickly?"

I had no idea what she was talking about, but in short order a group of villagers gathered around to explain that a manticore had been sighted in the vicinity the previous day. Fortunately, it hadn't killed any townspeople yet, but it had devoured four fenced-in goats. This was odd behavior. Manticores ordinarily prefer humans over livestock, but the beast's footprints suggested it was lame, and it had gone after the goats because they were easy meals.

The villagers had sent a messenger racing on horseback to the Royal Mews to request help. It would take two days for word to reach Babak, and another two or three days before a ruhker and roc would arrive. In the meantime, no one was allowed past the edge of the town. The residents were all indoors by sundown with their doors and windows boarded shut.

Now I was here. So was the manticore that had escaped Zahra only to kill Minu and nearly kill Darius. The one that had ruined Nasmin and caused her and Azar to be sent away in disgrace. The beast with one brown eye and one blue. The monster that was, it seemed, all my monsters in one.

At first light the following morning, I took Zahra out into the countryside where the manticore had been sighted. The monster's tracks from the destroyed goat pen led away into a long, shallow valley dotted with lonely stands of oak and cypress and expanses of brittle waving grass. All day long, I followed after it, guided by instinct. The manticore would've searched out shade among the trees and spent the middle of the day sleeping. Now, as the shadows lengthened in late afternoon, it would be rousing with a fresh appetite, thinking of food as it slunk back toward the village.

I stood in the chariot on a low rise looking downwind into a field with patches of sparse forest hunching on its sidelines. The manticore was here; I couldn't see it or hear it, but I could feel it. There were a hundred places it could hide among the dry vegetation and outcroppings of rock. I untethered and unhooded Zahra. She took in the surroundings with a few jerky movements of her head. She roused, took a crap, and launched herself into the air. As I watched her rise, I whispered in prayer, "This is for Darius and Minu, for Nasmin and Azar, for Mother and Arnan."

I whipped the horses and plunged the chariot through the grass. The carriage rattled violently under my feet and through my bones. The wind tore through my hair and whistled through my teeth as I opened my mouth and screamed in challenge, in rage and grief, in wild and defiant invincibility. The mouse calling the lion.

And the manticore came for me. It separated from the darkness between the trees and came running for the woman all alone, the one mad enough to be out near sunset, shrieking and heedless of death. From the side of my jouncing vision, I saw it gaining on me, but I felt no fear. The manticore's quilled pelt was matted with dried blood on one side. Its barbed tail was low to the ground and its shoulder blades jutted sharply from its back. The diabolical ape face was no less terrible to look upon, but the toothsome jaws lolled open not in grinning menace but a grimace of hunger and pain. Minu's talons had sunk into its left shoulder and the puncture wounds had become infected. Its limping stride was ungainly as it bounded as fast as it could for my chariot.

It was a pitiful sight. I'd feared and hated manticores all my life. Never once had I felt the slightest remorse when one of them died under my roc's talons. The manticore was a monster, but it was also an animal. An animal in pain. It needed to catch me. It needed to eat. And though it was natural for me to hate, I didn't hate it.

I didn't even look up. I trusted in Zahra the way one trusts in God. My horses were tired, laboring after long days of travel, their flanks lathered with sweat. The manticore put on a burst of speed, closing the gap. Glancing over my shoulder, I felt a strange calm as I stared into its mismatched eyes. Even though I was the prey, I held the power of life or death. Catch me and live. Fail and die.

Closer.

Closer. The beast's rancid, panting breath on my back, claws swiping for the wheels.

Zahra landed on the manticore's neck and drove it face-first into the ground. Did she know, I wondered, as my breath caught. Did she know this manticore had escaped her before? Does a roc live purely in the moment, or does she hold past failures in her heart as we do? Was it just another kill, or did she feel vindictive triumph as her talons sank into flesh?

The momentum of the tumbling monsters somersaulted them both end over end toward me in an avalanche of stabbing quills, teeth, and talons. The manticore screamed, a terrible rending shriek that I can never describe. Even the chariot horses, the bravest of their kind, trained not to react to rocs flying over their heads and manticores charging after them, whinnied and reared in terror at the sound and fury. I pulled them around sharply as the manticore's barbed tail whipped through the air, poisonous quills thudding into the side of the chariot. Zahra's foot sank into the manticore's face and her talons punctured its skull. My eyes were on Zahra and the manticore alone, so when the chariot wheel struck a rock at high speed, and the box went up into the air, taking me with it before hurling me back down, I didn't know what was happening, and for a second my mind stuttered with wonder that I had finally done it, I had become one with my roc at last. This was what it felt like to fly.

I was staring at the sky. I must've blacked out for a few seconds when I hit the ground because I had no memory of the impact or how I ended up underneath the chariot box. It was lying on its side on top of my legs, the left wheel still spinning. Slowly, I turned my head. The shaft had broken and the yoke snapped off when the chariot overturned. I could see the horses standing some distance away, tossing their heads and snorting in agitation, their harnesses hanging loose. When I turned my head the other way, I moved something else involuntarily and sharp pain shot through my trapped legs into my hips. Breathing through gritted teeth, I stared into the dead face of the manticore, a body's distance away from me. Zahra sat mantled atop her kill. She was calmly eating from the skull.

I tried to push myself out from under the chariot and immediately regretted it. Tears of pain sprang to my eyes. My left leg was pinned at a disturbing angle. Sprained at the very least, most likely broken. A wave of self-loathing crested over me. This is why ruhkers go out with a partner. This is why we turn back well before the sun goes down. Why we pin our name flag to the area we're hunt-

ing in on Babak's big map in the briefing room, so others
know where to look for us if we don't return.

Yet even in my terrible situation, I couldn't find it in
myself to regret the risk I'd taken. The manticore was
dead. The satisfaction of its death wasn't the gleeful ven-
geance I might've expected. I was glad it was dead because
it couldn't harm anyone else, and because it was out of its
misery.

I tried again to crawl out from under the chariot. If
I could get free, I could create a makeshift splint for my
leg and . . . then what? With a broken limb, I wouldn't be
able to right the chariot or reharness the horses and get
Zahra and myself back to the village we'd left behind that
morning, not before night fell.

One step at a time, I told myself. But I couldn't get past
the first step. My leg was pinned between the rock I'd run
over with the wheel and the bottom corner of the chariot
box. The pressure was just below the knee, so trying to
pull out of my boot wouldn't help. I strained to push the
chariot with my arms, but that barely budged it. Panting
and sweating, I fell back into the grass.

Zahra was still eating. She gorged herself until she was
heavy and full, then walked away and stropped her beak
against the grass. She tilted her head this way and that,
taking in the waning light, the untethered horses, and
the overturned chariot with me pinned beneath it. *Curious*, she seemed to be saying with her unconcerned stare.
Very curious.

"Zahra." A roc is not a dog that will run for help to save its master, nor even a horse that will return home with an empty saddle. Zahra hopped onto a nearby flat boulder, cleaned herself, then closed her eyes and went to sleep.

I resigned myself to the fact that I would need to be rescued. What other alternative was there? Could I use my skinning knife to amputate my trapped leg? Pain, fear, and blood loss would surely cause me to pass out long before I succeeded. I gathered whatever small stones were within my reach and threw them at the horses, hoping to drive them to return to the village, or to wander off in a direction that would lead to people who would notice their broken harnesses and investigate. The stones fell well short of their target. The disloyal steeds, hungry and tired from days of travel, sheltered under the shade of a tree and chomped at the grass. At the risk of attracting another manticore, I shouted long and loud for help. The sound carried across the wide plain and was swallowed by the sky.

The afternoon cooled into evening and then inexorably into night. Thank God it was not yet late enough in the year for the temperature to drop to freezing, but it was still too cold for me to sleep for more than a few minutes at a time, despite my exhaustion. I curled up to the extent possible, sheltered under the damnable chariot with my back to the wind and my arms wrapped around myself, shivering badly. My throat was parched and sore from yelling. I drank small sips from my waterskin, trying to conserve what I had. The night crawled by in a dull agony. Zahra was a feathery mountain in the dark.

Would this be how I died? The jaws of the manticore might've been preferable.

When the sun finally came up on my misery, carrion birds were circling overhead, drawn by the dead manticore, and a pair of jackals were stalking around, edging closer hopefully. Zahra hopped down from her low perch, spreading her wings and opening her beak menacingly. They slunk away. I couldn't see the horses nearby anymore; they had wandered off at some point during the night.

Zahra tore open the belly of the manticore and ate more of the carcass. As the air warmed, I couldn't escape the stench of meat baking in the sun. The manticore had been pregnant. I learned this when Zahra plucked out the gray foetuses and swallowed all three of them, one after the other. I had never seen a pregnant manticore before. In my unexamined imagination, the beasts spawned in the darkest depths of hell, springing to earth fully formed. But of course that was not true. They must mate and give birth, raise their young, feed them, protect them, and finally die as all living creatures did.

As the day dragged on, I grew weak and delirious. I still roused myself to shout for help, in the hope that someone might've seen the horses and would come searching, but my voice was noticeably weaker and my attempts grew more infrequent. This wasn't such a bad way to die, I decided. It was peaceful. The sky was a cloudless blue and the light was clear and warm. The pain in my leg had been fierce and throbbing at first, but now it was numb and, as long as I moved as little as possible, I couldn't feel my injuries. I was going out as a ruhker fulfilling my calling, having made one last dramatic kill. Once I was a corpse, wild animals would eat me and return me to the stream of life in which I had so happily waded. As a hunter, I'd taken so much life out of that stream, it was only right that I return to it in this way. And even now, at the end, I wasn't alone. Zahra was with me. By now, she'd eaten her fill of the manticore and didn't mind when the jackals returned to feed off the leftovers.

I watched her flying slow circles above me, the sun shining on the edges of her wings. Wait, no; I was confused. That wasn't Zahra. Zahra was still sunning herself on the rock. Another roc was in the sky.

Minu! No, Minu was gone. I didn't know this roc, had only for a second imagined that I did. The stranger dipped and drifted lower. A small roc, with brown banding across its chest, and no jesses.

I was gazing at a wild, male roc.

Zahra was gazing at it, too. She had never seen a male of her species before, one of her own kind flying free, far from chariot and ruhker. She stared up at the sight in rapt fascination. She didn't raise her wings in a threat display as she would've with another female. The male circled and circled, sailing lower and lower.

The moment before your life changes forever is crystalline. It stops your heart like a fly caught in amber. I recognized the sharp fear from years ago, when I'd faced Zahra's open crate.

"No," I croaked. "Zahra." My throat was the desert

and my words barely a whisper of wind over the sand. I called desperately upon those first dark days in the mews together, when my voice had been the line that stretched between us, binding woman to bird. I drew to myself the memory of every moment when it had been just the two of us, partners, sister monsters, when my voice was her constant, more than the chariot or the hood or the jesses or the meat, that tied her to the human world, to my will.

"Zahra," I rasped.

She launched herself upward. She was heavy with meat and her takeoff was full of effort. She pumped her powerful wings madly, the grass whipping beneath her maelstrom. It seemed for a moment as if she couldn't do it. She struggled to escape the earth, and I imagined it was me, my cruel but determined will that kept her grounded when it was clear in her heaving shoulders and piercing fixed gaze that she wanted to fly.

"I'm sorry," I cried, even as I stretched my hands to her helplessly. I was immobilized, injured, waiting to die. I had nothing to offer her anymore, but I didn't want to let her go. I still needed her. I needed her more than she needed me. That had always been true.

And then she was aloft. It seems impossible, when you think about it. How something so huge can conquer gravity. But we've always known that rocs are more than mere birds. There's a reason they're the subject of myths, why they adorn royal crests and are carved into the sides of temples. The fact that we ruhkers can hold these beasts to us is the unlikeliest of miracles, yet the miracle was everything I'd known and now it was leaving me. Zahra was leaving me, and my heart was dissolving into a thousand fragments.

"Don't go." I was shouting my whisper. I found the reed whistle around my neck and blew it, summoning her back to the chariot. At the sound, she seemed to hesitate, her attention torn by old habit. Then another broad stroke of her massive wings propelled her farther into the sky and away.

"Zahra. *Zahra.* Zahra!" A child's sob of abandonment and fear, a protest against loss too deep to comprehend and the heartlessness of the wild that had given me everything and taken everything away.

My roc flew after the young male. They rose upward together in perfect concert, already matched in height and speed and savage glory. She did not look back at me. I'd known she would not, yet still I wept and tried to fling my love out to her, to reel her back to me even as she soared to the horizon.

All at once it seemed, the fight left me. My tears multiplied, but I stopped calling to her. I saw her for the first time as she would've been if Gazsi had never taken her from the nest. If I had not penned her and tethered her, trained her and fed her, rode with her and loved her. She was my roc. She would always be my roc, even though she had never been mine to possess. I was alone again, but not empty.

"Thank you," I whispered, as she disappeared from my straining sight for the last time. For allowing me to hunt

with you. For letting me borrow your strength. For lend-
ing me your wings.

Alone, I waited for the jackals and vultures, for dehydra-
tion and hunger, for the impartial death that claims every
living thing at the end of its usefulness. When I closed
my eyes, I imagined a gentle tremor in the earth under my
back. The vibration of approaching hoofbeats. I turned
my head and saw through the waving yellow grass, ha-
loed by the light of the climbing sun, a horse and rider
galloping toward me. I smiled in recognition. It was the
ruhker in the field of my childhood home, the angel in
the gleaming red and black chariot calling down God's
attention with the reed whistle between his lips, gazing
at me with a laughing promise in his eyes. This time he
would reach out a hand to pull me up beside me and bring
me home.

Darius swung out of the saddle and fell to his knees
next to me. There was something different about his eyes;
it took me a moment to see the change. Gone was the flat,
sunken barrenness that had encased his features in winter
for all his days at the inn. His pupils were large with fear
and relief. They were alive, his searching eyes, the eyes
that danced across the horizon, that he shielded with his
hand when he gazed far off from the chariot. The eyes of
a man with something to live for.

"I saw Zahra fly," he gasped. "That's how I found you."

Darius found a stout branch to use as a lever and threw his weight against it, panting with discomfort from his freshly healed ribs. He pried the chariot off me and dragged me clear of the wreck. He examined my swollen leg and splinted it. He helped me drink, holding his waterskin to my cracked lips, then fed me flatbread and cheese from his bag. He explained that he'd left the inn a day after I'd departed, regretting that he hadn't gone with me in the first place. In the village by the river, he learned that I'd set off alone the previous day but not returned. He'd followed me. He'd tracked me as unerringly as he'd tracked quarry all his life. As I'd been calling for Zahra, he'd been searching for me.

He didn't ask about the dead manticore or the overturned chariot. We didn't talk about the roc-sized holes in our hearts. Instead, Darius lifted me carefully in his arms and set me on his horse, then got on behind me and held me steady against his chest, the gentle pressure like that of a ruhker's hands on a fledgling during their dark days, promising over and over—*you are with me now*. Together, we rode back toward the mews where, come spring, there would be new monsters to tame.

ACKNOWLEDGMENTS

Thanks go first and foremost to editor Jonathan Strahan, who convinced me to write a novella. He sat down with me over breakfast in Dublin during Worldcon 2019, when I was in the thick of penning an epic fantasy trilogy, and enticed me with the prospect of writing something considerably shorter. As it turns out, I had an unfinished side project I'd begun in 2015, at the time simply titled *The Roc*. After the convention in Dublin, my family and I spent a week vacationing in Ireland, during which we went on a guided hawk walk. Those two events gave me the impetus to finish writing the monster-hunting nature memoir that became *Untethered Sky*.

The team at Tordotcom has been wonderful to work with. Thank you to publisher Irene Gallo; in-house editor Emily Goldman; art director Christine Foltzer and interior designer Heather Saunders for making the book look so good; Jim Kapp and Lauren Hougen in production;

Amanda Hong, Deirdre Kovac, and Sam Dauer for copy-editing, proofreading, and cold reading; and the marketing, publicity, and social media gurus Julia Bergen, Caro Perny, Jocelyn Bright, and Samantha Friedlander for launching this book into the world.

Jaime Jones was the perfect choice of artist for the cover; I couldn't be happier with how he brought Ester and Zahra to visual life in such stunning fashion.

My appreciation as always to my agent, Jim McCarthy, for handling every business detail.

Thank you to E. J. Beaton, Sam Hawke, and Rowenna Miller for providing beta reads of the manuscript, and my gratitude especially to expert falconers Essa Hansen and Anne Heintzman for scrutinizing all the falconry details in the story. A shout-out to the Bunker, for the ample encouragement I needed to write something very different from my previous work.